A GOOD MAN

A GOOD MAN

by

Jefferson Young

THE BOBBS-MERRILL COMPANY, INC.

PUBLISHERS

Indianapolis   *New York*

813.54
Yo89

First Edition

28993
May '53

For
Clara and Shelby Young

A GOOD MAN

ONE

HE HURRIED, dodging the water in the puddles where the pig had rooted, and with each long step he took, his black rubber boots made little noises on the wet pasture grass. He moved easily and his steps were sure, though his shoulders felt tight beneath the faded denim jumper he wore. The coiled rope he carried dripped water onto the jumper's tail, and sometimes the dampness touched his bare skin and made cold streaks along the small of his back.

The road he followed across the pasture was an old one that he knew well, but today it appeared different to him. For he had determined to paint his house white and this decision was to be a turning for him. He slowed his gait and remembered the moment when he had told Louella about the house. He saw her face again and with the seeing he wondered if he would be able to get the house painted. He would, he told himself quickly, and hastened on to meet Cooter, who would be beyond the creek with the calf.

He had got the calf from Mister Walker, the one-armed dairyman who owned twenty cows. Mister Walker did not keep bull calves born to his herd, and he had offered the calf to Albert in exchange for four days' work of digging postholes for a new fence. Albert had accepted the work at once, and for two days he had been studying how he could best fit the calf into his plan. He had finally decided to keep the calf until he weighed two hundred pounds. He would sell the calf then, and save the cash until the fall of the year when the cotton was ginned. In the fall he would put the money he got for the calf with the amount he cleared from the cotton, and he would buy the paint. His heart quickened with the thought of that time and he nodded to himself, pleased that he had everything settled in his mind.

Just as he headed for a small path that led into the trees he heard a long wail come from behind him. He stopped and turned.

Back at the tenant house Daniel crouched in the kitchen door crying. Daniel was afraid of the old woman. Albert wished that he could talk to the boy, to tell him again there was no harm in her. But he

was too far away across the pasture; he motioned
Daniel back inside and went on again.

He smelled resin and damp cedar when he entered
the thin growth of trees that separated the pasture
from the creek. Beside the creek he paused to search
the opposite bank for his son. But Cooter was not in
sight and Albert studied the stream. The early spring
rain had stopped, but the water was swift and already
flush with the tops of the banks.

After a moment of watching a pine cone float past,
he made his way to a little opening, to stand beside a
tree to wait. The clouds in the far west had melted
away, and beyond the old cotton rows in the field
across the creek, through the slender trunks of some
trees, the sun sank like a great striped orange. Evening colors lighted the low western sky, but overhead, north and south, the sky still held the dark
clouds left after the rain.

The tree Albert paused beside was a pine, and it
stood alone in the clearing, the highest tree to be
seen for miles. It looked out on his fields, there where
the land rolled warm and pleasant as a woman. The
tree took its life from the same earth he tilled, and
through all the years when he stood beside it, resting
and thinking, a deep feeling of its strength had

grown over him. Now, slowly, he lifted his eyes to where the top branches spread out and upward against the sky, and as he looked he drew his shoulders back and stood more erect. Though he did not lean, he let his back touch the trunk, for today the tree appeared higher and stronger than ever before.

Once Mister Tittle had wanted to cut the pine for lumber. For a week Albert had begged him not to do it. With words that came slowly he had tried to explain to Mister Tittle what he himself did not fully understand. Mister Tittle had looked at him sharply and cursed: "Damn, Prince! Why in this hell-heated world don't you talk with sense?" But Mister Tittle had left the tree standing.

Sometimes as Albert rested the wind would stir the pine needles and they would whisper down a song to him. But today there was no sound, only the satisfied stillness of the earth in the hour after rain.

He tossed the rope aside and wondered if anything had happened to Cooter. Cooter had a boy's way with animals and Albert did not think his son would have any trouble with the calf.

It began to grow cool, and Albert fastened the jumper closer about him and tried to pull it down in the back. But it was too small for him; it would not come down. Mister John Mathis' store, where Albert traded on credit, did not carry odd sizes, sizes large enough for him. For three winters he had asked Mister Mathis to get a special jumper, but Mister Mathis lived in the fear of not collecting a debt and would never make the order. Often, when Albert left the store, he would hear the evening voices of the men who gathered there:

"Look at Prince Albert, folks. Look yonder how he high walkin."

A little smile would come to Albert's lips as he walked on unmindful, his shoulders back and the tail of the jumper flapping high about his waist.

He moved his feet now, and gazed impatiently across the water. He was seldom impatient and today he blamed it on his decision about the house. He had known from his father that in the life of every man there comes a day when he must finally stand for what he wants most, or give it up forever. He was glad, after his years of waiting, that he had brought himself at last to speak to Mister Tittle.

Dusk had begun to settle over the land before he suddenly took up the rope and moved toward the water's edge. Coming toward him across the cotton rows was Cooter with the calf.

"Is you got him?" Albert shouted.

"I got him, Papa."

Cooter came to the opposite bank and for a moment stood like a shepherd boy, the calf at his side and a stick in his hand.

"How come it took you so long?"

"We had to stop, Papa. Stop over there under a tree and talk some."

"Sho took you a time."

"Yessir."

"We got to hurry."

"Yessir, Papa."

"Head him on down to'ad the water. I going throw the rope."

Albert tied a piece of decaying tree root to the end of the rope and heaved it across the creek. It splashed at Cooter's feet.

"You be ticular, Cooter. That calf worth a heap to us. He worth four-five gallon of paint."

Cooter tied the rope about the calf's neck. "You ready, Papa?"

"Ready? I been here a whole hour being ready. Sho took you a time."

Cooter looked at Albert and grinned. "I gonna shove him in it, Papa."

14

"Ain't no need to shove that little fellow. You be ticular with him."

"Hey, calf," Cooter said. "Go on in it, now. This the time I told you bout."

The calf's front hoofs were at the edge of the water and now, balking, he tossed his white-spotted head high in the air.

"He s'pose to know whats to do," Cooter said. "But look like he don't." He turned to the calf. "We got to get on the other side, calf. You know that. Go ahead on, now."

The calf's nose quivered as he lifted a thin leg and put it out into the water. Then, balking again, he knelt on his front feet with his tail stiff in the air.

"Go on, now. Go on, now!" Cooter first coaxed, then demanded. "Go on off in it, calf!"

The calf did not move.

"Don't look like he gonna go, if'n I don't shove him some."

"That calf going be worth a heap to us, Cooter."

"He may is, Papa, but he don't hear me talkin. He understand whats to do." Cooter paused undecided a moment, then began to unlace his shoes.

"What you going do?" Albert said. "It gettin dark."

Barefooted now, his toes digging into the soft cold mud, Cooter threw his shoes across the water and began to unknot the rope.

"What you going do?" Albert said.

Cooter removed the rope from the calf and quickly put it around his own neck, knotting it firmly close against his throat. He waded off into the water.

"Make out I the calf, Papa. Pull!"

Albert stood braced, a little confused, and pulled, while on the opposite bank the stubborn calf knelt at the edge of the water as though in prayer. When at last Albert had the boy within reach, he leaned out and with one sweep lifted Cooter to the bank beside him. Cooter shook with cold and his full lips looked as though he had been eating blackberries.

"How you going get him now?" Albert said. "Just tell me that. Just tell me that, if'n you can."

Cooter shivered and tried to grin. "He comin, Papa."

They looked across the creek. The calf had already waded into the water and they watched him suddenly plunge into the current, his head high and pointed upstream.

"He comin," Cooter said.

"If'n he don't drown, he comin."

"He comin," Cooter said. He spoke as though to himself, and bent to put on his shoes.

The calf bleated and two little spurts of water shot up from his nose.

"He going make it," Albert said. "He going make it yet."

"Yessir."

"I do believe he going make it."

The calf pawed at the bank and Albert reached down to pull him up. "You all right, fellow. You here on the right side now. They ain't nothin going bother you."

The calf went to Cooter on tricky legs, found Cooter's hand and began sucking on one of his fingers. Cooter laughed. "He think I his mama."

"Both you-all going catch newmonias," Albert said, feeling sudden concern for them. "You got to dry yo'self."

The evening star came out bright and rode close upon their backs as they turned from the creek and headed across the pasture. Before them a thin strip of blue smoke rose, curling easily from the red clay chimney of the tenant house.

The house, and the sweet-gum tree near the lot, outlined themselves faintly against the dark sky. The house sat at the edge of the pasture. It was gray, like all the other tenant cabins that stood in lonely clearings about the countryside, and it was covered with a rusted tin roof that sounded loud and somehow comfortable when rain fell on it. The yard about the house was bare and hard, and at the front, near the water well, the naked branches of a peach tree laced the night.

"When you gonna sell him, Papa?"

"When he weigh two hundred pound. This calf going be worth a real piece of money."

"He sho pretty." Cooter put his arm across the calf's neck, and the calf, on his wobbling legs, followed the boy like a mindful child.

"We take him in to the fire," Albert said. "We get there, both you-all got to dry yo'self. You-all mighty cold, way you shiverin."

"Yessir."

"We get to the house, you dry yo'self," Albert said again, and all the time in the back of his mind he pondered how long it would take the calf to weigh two hundred pounds.

"I might die, Papa. This the season."

"What you say, Cooter-boy?"

"I say I might die, Papa. Preacher Tom say this the year for us colored folks to die. Preacher Tom say it on count of them dark nights durin Christmas. He say dark nights durin Christmas mean colored folks gonna die. If'n it be's white nights, mo white folks gonna die. Them was some mighty dark nights us had Christmas."

"Ain't nothin to that. Preacher Tom a good man, but sometime he carry some mighty queer notions in his head."

"He may could be right, Papa. He a preacher for the Lawd."

"They ain't nothin to that, now. We get home and get you and this bully dry. Then Mama give us some hot grits and meat."

They walked on, out of the pasture and to the lot, passing beneath the sweet-gum tree with its old gum balls like dark marbles. The lot was boggy, and at the stall where he would later put the calf Albert had to duck around a fallen end of the rotting roof. Through a big hole in the roof he could see more stars; the weather was clearing overhead. He hung the rope on a rafter, recrossed the lot and went through the creaking wooden gate. His stomach had already begun to rumble with hunger.

When he turned from the gate a low whimper came from the house and he saw a small dark form huddled in the doorway.

"Daniel?"

"Papa!" Daniel sprang across the yard. "Papa, I scared."

"Now," Albert said. "Now, now." He scooped Daniel up into the crook of his arm. "Don't you cry no mo, now."

"The old woman cuttin up, Papa. And just keep on and on."

"She ain't going hurt nobody." Albert leaned his head over to touch his son's, and kissed Daniel on the cheek. "She ain't going hurt nobody."

"I ain't scared no mo." Daniel clung tight to Albert's neck. "But I sho mighty hungry, Papa."

"We have us supper now."

"How we gonna eat, Papa? Mama ain't here."

Albert stopped in the middle of the yard. "Mama ain't in the house?"

"Nosir. She yet gone."

"Where she go to?"

"She gone to the road, talkin to peoples. Say she gonna go there and see who is all them peoples passin by."

Albert looked into the boy's face a moment before he went on across the yard. "She be back." He gazed through the back door into the kitchen.

The kitchen was dark except for pencil-sized streaks of light which shone through the cracks from the bedroom where the open fire burned. The streaks of light measured the stove into cold quarters. The kitchen was small, and the only other furniture it held was a bare board table, a chair with a broken leg and two wooden benches pulled beneath the table.

Albert put Daniel down on the step and went to the corner of the house to look northward toward the road and the store. At a distance the store lights flickered, and little twinkling spots lodged in his eyes. He turned to blink his eyes into the darkness, chasing the spots away, and went back behind the house.

"Mama comin?" Daniel said.

"She be back." Albert turned to help Cooter with the calf.

"You have to help him up the step, Papa. He ain't got no good legs yet."

"He a girl or a boy, Papa?" Daniel said.

"He a little bull fellow. And he cold."

Daniel suddenly pressed against Albert's leg, for just now, from a room beyond the kitchen, there came a low moan. The sound grew louder, and then louder, until soon it filled the house.

"Them nights durin Christmas," Cooter said.

"Ain't nothin to that," Albert said. "But it good we got the burial. Bring the calf on."

They entered the bedroom. The dying embers of the fire showed a bleak room with two double beds pushed into corners against the wall. In one corner stood a yellow straw broom worn stubby on the end, though the floor did not look as though the broom had been recently used. The walls of the room were lined with old newspapers and pieces of cardboard boxes. An end of cardboard beneath the closed shutter had been whipped free by the wind that had begun to rise, and the loose end flapped against the wall. Albert borrowed a tack from a higher spot and fastened the cardboard down again. Daniel was at his heels when he turned back to the fire.

The old woman gave out another moan from deep

in her throat. She sat far back in the corner of the
room. The deep folds of her sagging flesh fell layer
by layer about her and dim shadows moved near her
feet. Her withered hands were folded across her
shapeless lap, and she held her head angled to one side
and turned a little upward. She was Louella's grandmother and had come from the Delta to live with
them. She was too old to move about, so she sat
in the corner months on end, flabby and helpless,
with a deep-wrinkled face from which little black
eyes peered out. She had begun to moan two years
before, after the doctor had come with his pills.

Albert looked at her and shook his head and wished
again that he could do something to stop her suffer-
ing. The doctor had come three trips altogether and
Preacher Tom had prayed, but the old woman always responded more to her snuff than to their pills
and prayers.

"It good we got the burial," Albert said, and
turned to poke the fire with a stick.

"Sho make a heap of noise," Cooter said.

"She ain't going hurt nobody. You go head and
dry yo'self."

"Papa, Preacher Tom come here to see you,"
Daniel said.

"What the preacher want?"

"Say he wanna see you. Act like he ain't been talkin to nobody. Just whisperin round, like he do's."

"Low-talkin," Cooter said.

"Yessir. Say he wanna see you fo sho, Papa. Say it gonna be bad, don't he see you."

"He say he comin back?"

"Nosir. But he wanna know where is Lettie. Say he wanna find Lettie mighty bad."

"I take the calf, Cooter," Albert said. "Strip off yo clothes and dry yo'self."

"Ain't no use to strip, Papa."

"You strip them clothes off. You catch yo'self newmonias, stayin in them wet clothes."

Cooter removed his jumper and spread it out before the fire, but he made no motion to pull off his overalls.

Daniel made a face at Cooter. "You better mind Papa. You hear what he say."

"You ain't been gettin no calf with Papa," Cooter said. "You ain't been helpin him none."

"Pull them ov'alls off," Albert said. "Don't, you going be sick."

Albert squeezed water from the cloth onto the hearth and a cloud of steam boiled into the air. From

time to time, as he dried the calf, he paused to listen
for footsteps in the yard or on the lane that led to
Mister Tittle's barn and the road. And once he went
to the front porch and looked again toward the store.
When he came back into the room it seemed darker
than before and he went to the mantel and lighted
the coal-oil lamp.

The yellow glow of the lamp fell across the old
woman's face, showing the snuff stick, loose in the
corner of her toothless mouth, and the brown stain
of snuff juice that ran over her lips and down into the
deep wrinkles of her chin.

Cooter had turned his back to Albert and Daniel
and now he unfastened the straps and stepped out
of the overalls. He stood naked in the middle of the
floor, his young body smooth and gleaming in the
firelight.

"Dry yo both sides," Albert said.

"He shame, Papa." Daniel grinned. "Cooter shame
to turn round."

Cooter turned slowly. He did not look at Daniel,
or at Albert, but stood very still and gazed into the
fire.

Daniel sank back into the chair he sat in. "I wish
us had some cheese."

"We get us cheese on Sadday," Cooter said. "You know we get us cheese on Sadday."

Albert herded the calf toward the door. "Soon's I put this bully in the lot, I see can I get us supper."

"I sho hungry," Daniel said.

Albert had fed his sons fried corn bread and sirup and sent them off to bed. Now he sat before the fire with his hands folded between his legs. The wind outside had risen and he could hear it coming around the corner of the house, lashing through the big cracks of the wall and beating against the cardboard. He threw another piece of wood onto the fire. Tonight, more than in a long time, he wanted Louella beside him. He could not understand why she had not come home.

He stirred the fire again and thought of the calf that he had in the lot. The calf was a beginning for him this year. His thoughts excited him and he got up to walk back and forth before the fire. But the boards creaked beneath his feet and he was afraid he would wake Cooter and Daniel, so he sat down again and rested his head in the palms of his hands.

For a time he tried to figure in his head the gallons of paint that he would need for the house. But he found that he could not deal with numbers. He removed his boots and spread his toes to the fire, leaning back in the chair and listening to the wind and to the cry for more rain that came from the frogs in the pasture. His eyes closed and his head settled down onto his shoulders. He was comfortable, and lost in his thoughts, and he did not know how many minutes passed before he heard a step on the porch. His head snapped up.

"Mama?"

The front door creaked and closed and when he turned he saw her standing in the doorway. At her side, on the wall, a piece of newspaper fluttered and threw a fleeting shadow across her face. She came on into the room, toward the hearth. Her hair glistened and smelled of sweet pomade, and when she stood near, Albert saw the round spots of water that had splashed onto the skirt of her dress and the mud that caked the heels of her shoes.

"The rain gone," he said.

"I doubt it is," Louella said. "They a wind risin."

"I been hearin the wind. But they some stars showin."

"I spec it just waitin to get worser. Way things do."

27

He looked at her, but she had turned her head from him.

"You been to the sto?"

"I been up there a little while. Talkin to folks. They say the mill down again. Say Mister Dillard just ain't got no logs."

"You had yo supper?"

"I eat somethin with R-Rula." Louella sat in a chair and began to remove her shoes. "She ask me eat with her."

"I got me and them boys somethin," he said, without reproach.

"Them chillun in bed?"

"I reckon they sleep by now."

"You pay the burial?" she asked.

"I give the dollar to Jesse Darver." He glanced at the old woman. "It good we got that burial, hearin how she been moanin till just fo you come in. Where Lettie?"

"Sistah comin on with Augustus Brann." Louella smiled. "It sho somethin way he take on over her. Keep sayin, 'Come on here with me, girl. Leave that preacher lone.' And all the time Preacher Tom standin there stretchin his eyes lookin. Say he been on the road lookin for Sistah since way fo dark. I don't know what Sistah going do. . . . But she comin on with Augustus."

"We got the calf in the lot."

"Folks at the sto say Augustus sho mind them of you since he got back from the war. Say he growed up in the war."

"We got the calf in the lot," he said again, and patted his knees for her to sit.

"You damp," she said, and moved away to pull off her dress and fold it over a chair. This task finished, she crossed the room to shake the bed into order. Then she came back to the hearth and stood thoughtfully, gazing into the fire.

"You-all get the calf?"

"I told you, Mama. We got him safe in the lot. He a pretty calf, too. And he going be worth a heap to us, buyin that paint. Cooter brung him far's the creek."

Louella turned, and her shadow fell against the wall and moved leaning toward the corner of the room where the old woman sat. She took a comb from her hair and held it before her, inspecting it closely. "I wonder is you going be able to do it. They going be some mighty big folks wantin stop you. They sho is."

Albert smiled. "I don't think that, Mama."

"Well, Preacher Tom say he sho got to see you."

"I see him tomorrow."

Later, beside her in the bed, he pulled the quilt over them and put his hand across her waist. She was warm and soft to his touch, and they lay close and still for a long time before he lifted his head and leaned over to kiss her on the cheek. He was happy with her. And he was happy for the calf in the lot and for his sons and for his plans for the house.

But he could not sleep. He lay on his back and looked into the darkness. The sound of the old woman's snoring came across the room, and above the noise of the wind outside he heard a hundred frogs begging for more rain . . . more rain . . . more rain. . . . When he heard Louella breathing evenly he slipped from the bed and went to sit before the fire again. He sat quietly near the fading coals and thought of a younger night and his first crop with Mister Tittle. He had been filled with hope then, as he was tonight, for that had been a beginning for him, too. He stared into the coals, remembering.

TWO

ALBERT HAD COME to Longfield in the Piney Woods of Mississippi when he was seventeen, and through the years on the little farm among the pine trees he had forgotten much of his childhood near Grenada, where he had lived until his mother died with a fever. But he could still remember his father coming back from the church after the funeral and standing gravely with his hand on his chin.

"Don't you go in the house, son. Not no mo. It likely that fever catchin."

His father was a thin man who wore a neat goatee. He had lived in the Piney Woods as a child, before moving to the Delta. In the Delta the land was flat, shimmering and often unshaded, and he grew sad for the hills. He moved inland to Grenada and there met Albert's mother. Late in life they married. But Albert's father had continued to think of the Piney

Woods. He often spoke of moving back. Now that
Albert's mother rested among her people, Albert's
father stood with his back to the house, his arms
folded across his chest, and looked down the road.
Albert stood awkwardly, watching his father.

"We going, Papa?"

"Going in a little while. It best we go, like we been
thinkin. This place ain't going be the same no mo."

"You want me bring the wagon?"

"You get the wagon. And bring it round to the
porch. It best we go on this e'nin. That house full of
fever, and they say it catchin."

"Be sho you get that cap of mine, Papa. It hangin
there in the corner on a nail."

Albert looked through the door after his father a
moment, then went around the house to where the
old mule, already hitched to the wagon, stood tied
to a post. He led the mule to the front of the house
and waited until his father moved their furniture
onto the porch: a small cast-iron stove, three cow-
hide-bottomed chairs, two iron bedsteads with slats
and shuck mattresses, some pillows and patch quilts,
a water bucket and a dipper, a coal-oil lamp and a
small pile of clothes. Albert helped load it all into
the wagon.

"Here yo cap, son."

Albert put the leather hunting cap on his head and took up the reins. But his father remained standing on the porch.

"This all, ain't it, Papa?"

His father stood silently with his eyes fastened on the house. He stood as though lost in memory, with the sunshine on his gray hair and in his eyes a look of pain. Finally he came down the steps and got into the wagon.

"This all. We go on, now."

They headed south through September fields, traveling without haste, letting the mule set their pace. At night they stopped beside the road and slept on quilts beneath the wagon, and it took them three days to reach Jackson. They rode on, through country that unfolded in long stretches of low hills and where tall pines sometimes rose solitary against the sky.

To pass the time Albert would pick a high tree many miles ahead and make it their goal before they ate, before the sun went down, or for any other occasion his mind could invent to chop into small pieces the distances they traveled.

Once he saw a white house sitting against the green

foliage of a hillside; it was the finest sight Albert had ever seen and a sudden sensation came over him. He stood up, staring, and for a moment he lost his balance.

"What the matter, son?" his father asked. "You best mind you don't fall out the wagon."

"It pretty, ain't it, Papa?"

"What you see?"

"That house yonder. Sittin on that hill."

His father turned his head and looked at the house. "Sho is pretty. It look like a pitcher."

"Yessir, it do. It sho do."

Albert remained standing until the road turned and the house went out of sight behind them.

Soon they turned southeastward, going along a dirt road with high clay banks the color of ripe tomatoes. The pines grew thicker here and their tops moved with the wind. The country was thinly settled, and off both sides of the road, in open spaces, patches of brown straw swept backward to a distant rim of woods. Sometimes they passed lonely houses sitting in the center of unplowed fields, and twice they saw dogs beside the houses and once a man standing on a porch.

They rode on silently, until the sun went down and dusk began to deepen. Soon they came to a small

34

wooden bridge and a clear stream of water. And here they stopped to eat their supper. They sat on the sandy shoal of the creek, near a clump of huckleberry trees, and ate sardines and crackers and a piece of plain cake. When they finished they got down on their knees and drank cool water from the stream.

"Better make us a fire," Albert's father said. "We stay here tonight, and it likely get a little cool."

Albert gathered twigs and dry leaves while his father unharnessed and watered the mule. Then they spread their quilts on the dry sand beside the fire and talked quietly of Grenada.

"What you reckon Jubilee going do now, Papa? Now he ain't got no place to work."

"He say he going to Memphis. Say he ain't going work no place no mo. Jubilee just yo age, and he too young go runnin off to Memphis. It bad he picked a bad man to work with. He ought to knowed better'n do that. But then he young."

The moon had come up and its light sifted through the trees in small ragged pieces. The pieces clung to their backs like small tufts of cotton. The moonlight dappled the water.

"They say Memphis big," Albert said.

"They say it is," his father said. He looked into

the fire. "And Jubilee ain't going like it there. When a person settle down, he ought to find him a good man. Not do like Jubilee done. And find hisself in his fix. Some mens ain't bad. A person need to find him a good man, and then settle down with him. If he be's a hard worker, and steady with it, that man going stick by him, do things get bad."

"Yessir," Albert said.

"Jubilee young, but he ought to knowed better'n pick the way he done. But then he ain't. And now he lost his crop and movin off."

"He ain't going be up to Memphis long."

"I don't spec he is." His father lay down and rolled himself up in his quilt. "They some mo cake in the shoe box. You don't eat it, the ants be at it fo mornin."

Albert ate the cake and sat beside the fire with his hands locked around his legs. At his feet the stream gurgled quietly, and sometimes, off to his left, a bird darted about in the dry underbrush. And from far away down the creek came the faint hooting of an owl. Albert sat thoughtful a long time, watching the fire die away. When it was out he lay beside his father, lay with his head resting in the crook of his arm, and he fell asleep thinking of his father's words.

36

They were on their way again at break of day. They rode along the rutted road, and the sun came up and the air was dry and pine-scented. Where they rode now red gullies ribbed the bare clay hills. Here, in occasional patches, the land grew gum and hickory and beech and oak and elm, but it was scrubby pine that stretched as far as the eye could see.

Soon they came to Pearl River, but they did not cross it. They turned southward and rode for hours more, and it was late afternoon when they reached Longfield.

Longfield was a small town that contained a big general store and a sawmill. It was bordered on one side by a dusty road and on the other by a railroad track. The sawdust pile beside the mill was the largest thing in town, and just now some children could be seen tumbling down it in swirling clouds of red. The big houses of the whites cluttered loosely around the store, and from this center, beyond a breathing space of idle land, the town spread outward to gray tenant cabins, small farms and, farther on, the wooded stretches which fed the sawmill.

One of the first things Albert saw upon entering Longfield was a white house that sat on a knoll beyond the sawmill. A sudden sensation came over him again as it had on the road. He stood up, holding the reins so tightly that the mule stopped.

"Better not stop him here in the road," his father said. "Better pull him off to the side."

They stopped the wagon beneath a sweet-gum tree in front of the store. Three men sat on the store porch and Albert's father went over to ask them about a place to spend the night.

"You-all just comin here, ain't you?" one of the men asked.

"We is," Albert's father said.

The man nodded again. "I has a bed at my house they ain't nobody usin."

"We sho be much-oblige."

"Yessir," Albert said.

The man was Preacher Tom Snell. He did not say any more, but got into his car and drove down the road slowly, so that they could follow him in the wagon.

The following day Albert's father rented a two-room cabin across the tracks on the edge of Mister Dickens' farm. The house had not been used for three years, and before Albert and his father moved in they had to patch a hole in the roof and clear the briers away from the door.

"But it do for us," Albert's father said. "And it mo'n hold the things we got."

A week later Albert went to work for Mister Loomis at the sawmill. But all the time he worked he kept his eyes on the house at the end of town and the farm that lay behind it. One day he asked his father to go to the man who owned the house, to see if he needed someone to make a crop. It was December and Mister John Tittle did not need anyone.

"But he going need somebody fo long," Albert's father said. "You get a chance, you move on with Mister Tittle. I hear tell he first deacon in the Baptist Church. And he cusses better'n anybody I ever heard. You get you a chance, you move on with him."

"He look like he got a good place," Albert said.

He worked on at the mill. He arose at five-thirty every morning, and when the sawmill started at seven o'clock he began lifting the green cuts of lumber and stacking them beside the mill to dry. He worked all week until Saturday at noon, when he collected his pay. On Saturday nights he went to the store with his father to buy groceries, and once a month he had his hair cut by Old Reuben. Sometimes his father went home early, while Albert went rabbit or possum hunting, or remained at the store talking to the other boys who gathered there. One summer night after his father had gone home Albert met Louella.

A group of boys was standing in a circle out beneath the sweet-gum tree. Albert heard their laughter, and their sudden silence, and he thought they must be watching a crap game. Near them, he heard the soft clapping of their hands. He moved to the edge of the circle, and over their heads he saw a girl dancing in a yellow dress. She had removed her shoes and she danced on the soft grass barefooted. She had laughing eyes and pretty teeth, and when she whirled the wide skirt of her dress fanned upward. Albert clapped his hands with the others. Once, briefly, his eyes met the girl's. But she turned on, swiftly, again and again, until Albert was dizzy from watching her. Then she stopped. She looked quietly at the boys around her and said, "Now who going buy me a pop?"

"A pop, Louella?"

"A soda pop. Who going buy me it?"

"Aw, go on, now."

"Go on? Don't say go on. Say here yo drank."

"I ain't studyin no drank."

"Come on, now. Buy me a pop."

"I ain't got no money, girl."

She put on her shoes and started away, and when she passed near Albert he said, "I get us a drank."

She stopped, smiling and breathless, and looked at him. "What yo name is?"

"Albert," he said. "Albert Clayton."

They went into the store and Albert bought two cold bottles of orange soda. And that night he walked home with her.

The next morning his father said, "You get any rabbits last night?"

"Nosir, Papa. We ain't hunt none last night."

"You been come in mighty late."

"Yessir. After you left, I stayed round the sto jo'-ree'in with them folks."

"You ain't got nothin to do, we go over there and see Uncle Scott. They say he ain't been able move bout much."

When they passed Mister Tittle's house Albert said, "It a good house, ain't it, Papa?"

"It pretty," his father said. "And I s'pose it mean mo'n just a white house. What time them folks leave the sto last night?"

"It been going on twelve o'clock fo they left. They stayed round there mighty late."

They left the road and crossed a fence and walked through a growth of trees. The shade was thick as early dark and their feet came down softly on layers of leaves.

"What it mean, Papa?"

"What what mean, son?"

"The house. Mo'n just a house."

"I s'pose it mean somethin inside folks. Somethin I ain't found, and my folks ain't found, and they folks on back. But likely you going find it."

They went out of the woods, to where the sun was bright and the air was cool and birds were in the sky.

"I do believe you going find it," Albert's father said again. He breathed heavily from the walking. "Every man meet a day when he got to cide, one way or a t'other, for what he want. I believe you going be ready when the day come."

"Yessir."

"It going make me proud to know you found us place at last."

They reached Uncle Scott's house and knocked on the door. The slow shuffling sound of feet came from behind the door and a chain rattled a long time before the door opened and Uncle Scott came out.

He was wrinkled and stooped and glad to see them and they sat on the porch.

Albert's father and Uncle Scott talked of many things, of old times, and Albert listened, but after an hour he grew restless and at last he said, "Papa, I think I go down the road a piece."

"Where you going off to, now?"

Albert did not look at his father. "Just down the road, Papa. I ain't going be gone long."

His father's eyes twinkled and he shook his head. "Get on, then. Get on. But member you got yo work tomorrow."

Albert knew that his father's and Uncle Scott's eyes followed him when he walked away. And when he glanced back he saw them nodding their heads to each other, as though sharing some secret. He walked on, down the road to visit Louella, but he went home before dark. And at seven o'clock the next morning he was at the sawmill ready to work again.

His days at the sawmill passed quickly. Summer passed and winter came. Mister Loomis could not buy enough logs because of the heavy rains, and some days Albert did not work. Then spring came, and one day his father appeared at the sawmill.

"I seen Mister Tittle," he said. "He say he going

need somebody for a crop. You go see him when you get off from yo work."

Albert asked Mister Loomis to let him leave before five o'clock, and early in the afternoon he walked toward the white house.

Mister Tittle stood in the yard, a wiry man with black hair and black eyebrows and flashing eyes.

"E'nin, Mister Tittle," Albert said.

"Good evening." Mister Tittle squinted into the early-afternoon sun, then looked at Albert again. "How old are you, boy?"

"Going on nineteen, Mister Tittle."

"Goddamn. You mean to say you're eighteen?"

"Yessir."

"Water for the saints in hell! Then say you're eighteen. Are you married?"

"Nosir. But I courtin Louella some."

A smile touched the corners of Mister Tittle's mouth. "Courting a gal, are you? Well, I'm a sonofabitch!" He looked at Albert and his eyes flashed. "What're you doing that for, boy?"

Albert hung his head. "Nothin, Mister Tittle."

"A woman is the goddamndest last thing on this devil's earth you could need," Mister Tittle said, and glanced behind him toward the kitchen. The smell of frying ham was on the air.

Mister Tittle raised his voice again. "This is hard earth, boy, and it takes a willful man to get his living from it. The farm I have here is small, and slow-dying. It's about a hundred and ten acres of pasture, sandy loam and good bottom land. Are you willing to work hard, boy?"

"Yessir."

"Can you run fast?"

"Sir?"

"I say can you run fast?"

"Yessir, Mister Tittle. I swift on my feet."

"Well, damn-it-to-hell, don't stand there on your long legs and stare. Start running. Run hard as you can. If that girl you're after will have you, go ahead and move in. It's March, and there's work to do."

"Yessir, Mister Tittle. Yessir." And Albert ran all the way to Mister Barlow's farm where Louella lived.

They were married by the justice of the peace beneath a pecan tree beside the courthouse at the county seat. They stood awkwardly with the sunshine in their faces and during it all Albert was not able to keep his eyes off the red-brick jailhouse at his right. When the ceremony was over they went behind the jailhouse and drank artesian water from a limp stream flowing through a bent copper pipe. Albert let Louella drink first. And before they got into the wagon to ride the seven miles back to Longfield, he bought her a pink rayon slip and a red-checkered gingham dress. That same afternoon they moved onto Mister Tittle's farm.

Cooter came that first year. The birth of the boy filled Albert with joy, and he worked harder than ever before. He entered the fields when the whippoorwills came and he gathered his crops when October leaves began to fall. The seasons came and passed. The sawmill moved away one summer, but another one managed by Mister Dillard came to take its place by spring. The years slipped by in their order, and when Cooter was six years of age and Daniel came, Albert was twenty-five, and it seemed to him he had always lived in the Piney Woods.

Cooter cried when his brother was born, and ran out of the house. Albert led the boy back inside and to the bed to look at the baby. The child looked all hands and feet, and Cooter said, "He look funny,

46

Papa. He look just like that little pig belong to Mister Tittle."

The baby kept on crying. Cooter lifted him into his arms and went to rock his brother in a chair, cooing down at him, "You hush this fuss. You hush up, now." Rocking back and forth easily, saying, "Where all that racket comin from? And you lookin xactly like that little pig belong to Mister Tittle. You hush up, now."

The baby quieted and Cooter grinned. "He little, ain't he, Papa?"

"Sho is," Albert said, and for a long time he stood above his boys, watching them and feeling proud.

During the months that followed, Albert often sat on the porch at evening while twilight settled over the land. He would hold Daniel on his knee and look up the lane toward the house on the little rise. Sometimes he caught himself staring.

The house was a frame one, small and neat, and it looked cool on the hottest days. The back of it faced down the lane, across the pasture to the creek and to the fields beyond. Once Albert went inside the house. He walked lightly, though it seemed to him his steps thundered. In one room he stopped and stood very

47

still for a long time while he drew in deep breaths, wanting the clean smell of the rooms to enter him so that he would never forget. He lifted his feet carefully and moved on. When he passed into the living room he dared to touch the flower-patterned brocade cover of a big couch which sat against a wall beneath a big picture of a ship at sea. He trembled as he went out into the yard again; and he kept walking lightly, as though still on the carpeted floor.

Several days after his visit into Mister Tittle's house the old woman came. No one had known she was coming. Preacher Tom found her wandering along the road with a paper bag under her arm. She refused his offer to ride, so he parked his car and led her down to Albert's house.

"I here," the old woman said as they gathered about her. She carefully placed the paper sack in a corner beside a chair.

"We put her in the room with us," Louella said. "She my gran'mama from the Delta."

"I here," the old woman said with a heavy sigh, and sank into the chair beside the paper bag.

Albert did not mind the old woman: she was Louella's grandmother from the Delta. He bought her a jar of snuff once a week and gave her the special attentions due her age. The old woman proved to be company for Albert's father; though she said little, he often engaged her in long and pointless conversation, speaking as old people will. As the months passed, Albert and Louella accepted her presence as if she had always lived with them. . . .

One afternoon of a long summer day the following year Albert sat looking up the lane. His porch faced Mister Tittle's house and he suddenly felt the need to stand up, to move about. With Daniel clinging to his neck, he left his chair and strode up and down the porch with his head going round. The feeling of restlessness passed and he went to the lot to get some corn to shuck and shell to take to the gristmill on Saturday. His father was on the porch when he returned. Albert saw the drawn wrinkles about his father's eyes and the grave expression on his face.

"Where you been, Papa?"

"Over in the back field with Cooter. We went over there, but we took us time."

"Come draw me some water," Louella called from the kitchen.

"Comin in a minute," Albert's father said.

49

"I get the water, Papa," Albert said.

"You go on with shellin the corn. I least can help Louella some."

Albert's father took the bucket from Louella and went to the water well beyond the peach tree. Albert watched his father, noticing the tired movement of his father's arms as he pulled on the rope. When his father came back into the shade of the peach tree he stopped and rubbed his hand across his face, as though to clear his eyes. His knees sagged. Albert ran across the yard. But before he reached the peach tree his father had slumped to the ground.

"Papa?" Albert lifted his father's head onto his knees. "Papa?"

But his father did not answer and a few moments later he was dead. Albert lifted him and carried him inside to a bed. His father's face showed strength even in death, and before Albert pulled a quilt over him he reached down and touched the little goatee as he might touch a child's face. After he had sent Cooter for Preacher Tom, he walked out of the house and across the pasture to the creek and stood beside the tree in the clearing. He stood sadly, with his arms folded and his back resting against the tree. Darkness closed about him and the stars came out.

But he did not stir until he heard Cooter calling him.
His son came to the clearing.

"Papa? Papa, Mama say come on to the house. Say
folks a-comin."

Albert put his arm across Cooter's shoulders and
they walked slowly, silently, back to the house.

THREE

THE DAY FOLLOWING the funeral, Albert made arrangements with Mister Wiggins at the county seat to pay for his father's casket. The casket cost a hundred and twenty dollars, and two years passed before Albert was able to make the final payment. But once out of debt for it, he wasted no time in signing for the burial insurance policy with Jesse Darver.

He hurried home to show the policy to Louella, but she did not answer when he called at the door. He looked through the house and from the kitchen he caught sight of her out in the garden picking collards. He crossed the yard, calling to her, but she did not look up until he came through the garden gate.

"You get the burial?"

"I got it, Mama."

"I glad you is. Them folks up yonder yet talkin bout that funeral. And it two year gone. Mister Dil-

52

lard and them know you just paid the coffin off. Sistah come by here this mornin sayin she heard Miss Dillard and Miss Mathis in the sto talkin."

"What they sayin?"

"Sistah say they sayin it just like us folks to pay all that for the funeral. And all the time ain't had nothin fittin t'eat. Sistah say it Miss Dillard and Miss Mathis talkin. Up at the sto. And both them white womens got them big cars to ride in."

"Don't you pay them no mind, Mama."

She snapped the brittle collard leaves with quick, angry movements of her hand. "Ain't they business how we spend us money. Or how us go in debt. Ain't none of they business a-tall. They just ain't no use folks being like they is."

"Don't you pay them no mind."

He helped her pick the collards, which she put into her apron. Behind them the sun was already beyond the pine trees.

"Where them boys?" Albert said.

"They on that creek again. They don't stay way from it, they going both fall in. I told them chillun stay way from the creek, but they go right on. Cooter ain't never here to draw me no water. And when he bout the house he lookin at that Bible. He going look

53

at that book till he go slap-silly in his head. Lessen
he fall in that creek first. And they moccasins on
that creek big as bean poles."

Albert put his arm around her waist and they
walked to the end of the row of collards and on into
the yard.

"I get you some water."

"I done got the water myself. Best you get them
chillun on back to the house."

He pinched her ear lightly with his fingers.

"Stop that! You got to find them chillun!" She
pulled away from him, laughing, clutching the collards tight against her stomach, and ran up the steps
into the kitchen.

Later, when supper was over, Albert went out to
the porch and sat looking up the lane. He sat quietly,
listening to the chirping of the crickets and watching
the fireflies flick their quick light through the darkness. He had thought a lot during the year, and he
had begun to take a dream about with him, like a
woman big with child. During the winter while cutting logs, and during spring while breaking land, he
nursed his thoughts to himself. But by fall, when he
was gathering cotton, he sometimes found himself
going about in a daze.

"Lord God," Mister Tittle said one day while they harnessed the mule. "Lord God Almighty, Prince. You've put the collar on backwards. You've been acting lately like you're eighteen and in love again."

"Yo house sho pretty, Mister Tittle."

"Just a white house, Prince."

"Yessir." He looked down the lane toward the tenant house. "They been somethin———"

"Damn!" Mister Tittle shouted. He jerked his hand back from the harness trace he had been hitching.

Albert turned his head to hide a grin, and that day he did not try again to talk seriously with Mister Tittle.

Two weeks later Albert sold his cotton. And when the corn was gathered and the fences patched he went to work cutting logs for Mister Dauber. A month later Lettie moved into Albert's house. She was Louella's sister, and she did not want to go with their stepfather when he left Mister Barlow's farm to move to another down near the county seat.

Winter came, December passed, and the quick cold days of January held the land before Albert's thoughts grew too heavy for him to bear. One day when he stood at the barn with Mister Tittle he knew the time had come for him to speak again.

"I like to paint my house white, Mister Tittle."

He could not look at Mister Tittle when he said it, but watched some red hens behind the barn as they pecked at some corn.

"Well, damn, Prince," Mister Tittle said. "Well, goddamn."

Mister Tittle pulled his coat close about his waist and stood as though at a loss for words. His eyes were bright as always, and above them now little furrows creased his forehead as though chiseled there with a knife. He looked at Albert steadily while he slowly took a handkerchief from his pocket and wiped his chin. Finally he said, "Hell, Prince. What for?"

"It dreary, Mister Tittle. It just dreary."

"Horse manure," Mister Tittle said.

Albert's thoughts began to have sound then, and because he had never dared give them voice, he spoke hesitantly, fearing words would stifle him.

"Yessir, it is. But it mo . . . it mo'n that. It somethin been with me a long time. It been . . . since back yonder . . . back yonder when I come to the Piney Woods. Maybe even fo I bo'n, cause it

56

been with Papa. It somethin he use to say. He say it go back to his papa, and his papa's papa, and then on back some mo.

"Yo house pretty there on the little knoll. It pretty like some the other houses in this town. And could I paint that house of mine, I believe . . . I believe I be going to'ad somethin. Somethin Papa and his folks on back been lookin for and ain't found. A white house let a man be a man."

He stopped and looked far away beyond the tenant cabin to an indefinite spot where the pine trees stood deep against the winter sky.

"A white house let a man be a man."

His desire was deep and he knew that it came from the toil of an earth his father's father had always known, and his father's father's people on back. His father had always spoken vaguely about it, as though it was something that came from so far back it was a little beyond them all.

"I sho like to paint it."

"There's not a tenant house around here painted white," Mister Tittle said.

"Yessir."

Albert watched Mister Tittle gaze across the land. They had worked in the fields side by side, each of them respecting the other's labor, and through the years a silent sharing had grown between them. It was a quiet and voiceless bond, and it came to them from the land they tilled.

Mister Tittle looked across the land as though remembering the good years and the bad years he had shared with Albert. Albert stood waiting, watching Mister Tittle, remembering the other's face in a hundred moods but never before so stilled.

Mister Tittle suddenly shook a fence post as though in anger and wheeled toward Albert with his eyes flashing.

"There'll be talk. And the Lord alone knows what else besides talk. But you want to paint it?"

"Yessir. Somethin make me want to paint it mighty bad."

"The Lord only knows . . ." Mister Tittle struck the fence post a blow. "I won't be able to help you any. It's something you and Louella'll have to do yourselves."

"Yessir. That just the way I want it. I like us do it just usself."

"You'll have to buy your own paint and do your own job of painting. But that house down there is mine. It's on land I bought and paid for. And you can paint it if you think you can.

"But if something starts about it, don't look to me. If something starts, remember it's your business all around."

"Yessir," Albert said quickly.

"Then paint it if you can. But I wouldn't go hollering up and down about it. People are going to know you're doing more than painting a house. And they'll talk. It's not the talking I mind. But if it's more than that . . . Where're you going to get the money? You didn't clear but forty-three dollars in the fall. You may not do that good this year. How're you going to do it?"

"I going work and save for it," Albert said. "I going start to save for it." In his joy he turned abruptly and walked off down the lane.

"Prince," Mister Tittle called.

Albert stopped and looked back.

Mister Tittle shook his head. "Nothing. Never mind."

FOUR

ALBERT AWOKE to the sound of the wind. He lay still, listening to it whistle softly around the house and about the chimney. Then, easily, he stretched himself. When his eyes were full open he looked at Louella beside him, and moved his head and let it rest lightly against the warmness of her back. But he did not wake her now. He carefully tucked the covers about her and stepped onto the floor to dress in the cold without lighting the coal-oil lamp.

At the crumbling hearth he knelt before gray ashes which stirred beneath the faint breath of wind that came down the chimney. He made a clean round spot on the hearth and struck a match to fat pine splinters. Soon the kindling spewed and crackled, and when he put oak limbs across the splinters the fire threw patches of orange light across the floor.

Through these, without waiting to warm himself, he tiptoed from the room.

He found the calf awake and leaping about with hunger. He rubbed the white-spotted head. "I come back I going bring you some milk. We going get you some from Old Bertha. Ain't going be long."

He left the lot and started toward the lane, heading for Mister Tittle's barn to milk and to feed the mule.

The lane rose before him narrowly, like a long cut of new lumber pressed against the earth. The earth itself, beneath the darkness, lay ready to wake, and he thought of the morning as a deep breath drawn in and held, and in the full stillness the tread of his boots sounded loud against the ground. It was this quietest hour around the clock, this final hour before the sun came up, which he liked more than any other. For it was a time when, full of morning energy, he could without haste muse on the day's work ahead of him. As he went through the gate that led to the barn the faraway sound of a baying dog rose on the air.

With his familiar banging of the crib door Old Bertha stirred and lowed quietly, and he heard in the boggy lot the sucking tread of mule hoofs moving up behind him.

After he shucked the ears of corn and fed the mule he went into the stall where the cow stood with her waiting head thrust toward him. He milked with both hands and a thin warm steam drifted up from the pail into his face. Before the pail filled to its usual depth he put it aside and milked the strippings into a quart jar. He hid the jar in the crib behind a sack of feed, took up the milk and left the barn. Day was breaking and in the early light he stopped to look at the milk in the pail a long time before he went on to the kitchen door and knocked for Miss Mary.

Miss Mary was a fine woman who never nagged Albert with small chores about her house. And in all the years Albert had lived on Mister Tittle's farm he had never seen Miss Mary around the barn. But he had seen the butter she churned from the milk. Miss Mary took pride in her butter and always patted it into a wooden mold that left on the top the figure of a dainty little flower with two pointed leaves.

Albert heard her quick steps as she crossed the kitchen and came to the door.

"Good morning, Albert."

"Mornin, Miss Mary." He tried hard to think of something more to say.

"Mornin," he repeated.

Miss Mary took the pail and he turned to leave, without waiting to see if she would take note of the milk.

"Albert?"

He thought quickly and stopped and turned. "Yes'm?"

"Old Bertha won't get across the creek and not be able to get back tonight?"

"No'm. No'm, Miss Mary. I going keep her in the little pastah till the creek go down."

He went on to the crib to get the quart of strippings. Back at his own lot he poured the milk into a pan for the calf. He smiled at the calf's greed and remained beside him, watching him eat, sometimes talking to him. But soon pink and red colors flashed upward over the tops of the eastern pines and he went to the kitchen.

Louella bent before the stove, poking wood into the firebox. She did not look up at him and for a fleeting moment he saw an expression on her face which he could not define. But when she turned, and the light from the fire covered her, the expression vanished.

"You reckon I ought to go see what Preacher Tom want?"

"He say he comin here. Act like he want to see you mighty bad."

"I told him bout the house. Just him and Mister Tittle know. Mister Tittle say ain't no need go round talkin bout it, and Preacher Tom say he won't be tellin folks. Ain't they knowin I mind. It just it don't seem right shoutin it up and down the road. Wonder what the preacher wantin."

"He ain't said. Just say he got to see you."

Albert pictured the preacher driving his old car at exactly fifteen miles an hour, day in and out, over rough road and good, his face serious as he went about the countryside selling the line of cosmetics and flavors he bought from a wholesaler in the adjoining county.

"Preacher Tom a good man," Louella said.

"He is," Albert said. "I show him the calf, he get here. He be glad to know I got the calf."

The sun was like a flame over the land, and while Albert stood chopping wood beside the house he paused from time to time to glance up the lane. But it was after ten o'clock when Cooter shouted from the front porch. "Yonder he come, Papa. Comin down the lane."

Albert leaned on the handle of the ax and waited for the car to come to a stop beside the woodpile. Preacher Tom sat in a semicircle over the steering wheel, and behind the long thin cracks of the window glass his little eyes looked as though they had been stitched into his face by a dark-threaded sewing machine. He nodded, and his lips moved.

"Mornin, Preacher Tom."

Albert waited patiently, for he respected the preacher. He knew that for twenty years the preacher had never missed a sermon at his church. Though he misquoted the Scripture, and many of his congregation complained that he sometimes veered from the Word of the Lord altogether, he visited the sick and buried the dead and managed to find new subjects for his sermons.

But in recent years his voice had grown weak, and only the members who sat on the front benches could hear him. Those who did not hear came as always, to sit far outside the reach of their preacher's voice. They sat with their heads moving slowly, and when the collection plate was passed among them they dropped in their nickels and their dimes.

"Get out, Preacher Tom. Daniel say you come by."

Preacher Tom uncoiled himself from around the steering wheel and stepped out of the car. He stood tall as a rail, with a fringe of gray hair along his temples, and he looked at Albert with his little eyes. "Mornin, Prince."

"What that?" Albert leaned toward the bony face, where the skin clung tight against the high cheekbones.

"I say it a fine mornin, after all that rain."

"Sho is. I sorry I ain't been here last night. Me and Cooter been gettin a calf cross the creek."

"Louella say you gettin it." Preacher Tom nodded his head gravely. "Say you gettin the calf and makin yo plan to go on with what you told me bout."

"That calf going help a heap. And then when I gin the cotton, I be ready."

"Prince, I been done some thinkin since you told me what you plannin. I been thought a lot. Last night I spoke with Louella and I told her I sho want to come talk with you. I don't know if'n you ought to do what you aimin."

"How you mean that?" Albert said. He sat on a round block of wood and looked at the preacher. "How you mean that, Preacher Tom?"

Preacher Tom shook his head from side to side.

"We been give enough troubles, just the way things is. You know that already, Prince."

"I ain't going make no trouble."

"But they likely be some, you go on with things. They some white folks in this town going see you meanin mo'n just paintin yo house. They going see. They sho going see it. And they ain't going like that. Now, they ain't. It seem to me like we just got to take the ways we find. Even when they bad."

Albert looked off across the pasture while he turned the preacher's words over in his mind. Finally he said, "It seem to me like folks like to see a man do the best he can, Preacher Tom. They like to see him make a good crop, and grow fat hogs to kill, and fix things up. Far's I can see, that the way folks is."

"Sometimes they is, Prince. But then sometimes they ain't. Way it look to me, we s'pose to do like we is. We got us purpose, way all folks is."

"But they somethin make me want it dif'ent. It somethin Papa used to talk bout. He say it go back to his papa, and his papa's papa, and his papa's papa's folks on back. Ain't no notion I took sudden."

"Yo Papa been a good man. But I doubt he——"

"Yessir. He say his folks ain't found they place,

67

and they folks on back. But I going live here. This place home to me. And I hopin it to be home for them boys."

"I just want you know what I been thinkin, Prince. So's you can think bout it. It sho somethin fo you to put yo head on."

Albert thought of the pine tree beside the creek. He wanted to go to the little opening now, but he knew that he must not walk away and leave the preacher. After a moment of silence he left the wood-pile and walked with Preacher Tom to the front porch where Cooter sat.

"Prince, they some words in John you likely know. Words that say take my yoke upon you and learn of me. Them some pretty good words for folks."

Cooter grinned. "Ain't that in Matthew, Preacher Tom? Ain't them words in Matthew eleven twenty-nine?"

"The Holy Word," Preacher Tom said.

"Yessir."

"Cooter can sho member that Bible," Albert said.

Preacher Tom did not act as though he heard Albert. "How the old woman gettin long, Prince?"

"She ain't been doing so good, Preacher Tom."

"Sho ain't," Cooter said.

"Them dark nights us had Christmas," Preacher Tom said, and shook his head.

"And her moanin like she done yestiddy," Cooter said. "Moanin worser'n I ever heard her moan. It sho good we got that burial."

Just now Lettie appeared in the doorway. Her full face still held the softness of sleep and she walked slowly when she crossed the porch to sit beside Cooter.

"Sho a fine day, Lettie," Preacher Tom said.

"Seem like it is."

"You want to go ridin in the car?"

"I don't reckon I want no ride today."

Preacher Tom coughed. "I got to go down yonder and take Myrabell some stuff she sunt word for," he said to Albert. "But I be back this e'nin, Prince."

Albert went out to the woodpile but did not cut any wood. He looked across the pasture and did not know how long he sat before he heard Louella calling him. She stood in the kitchen door staring at him strangely, and when he neared the steps she said, "I been call you six-seven time. Ain't you heard me callin? Yo dinner on the table."

"I ain't heard you, Mama. But I ready."

They ate corn bread and fried meat and molasses. Albert ate slowly and he had not finished when Daniel and Cooter left the table. The boys did not leave the kitchen, but hung in the door a long time before Cooter said, "Papa, me and Daniel wanna go play in the sawdust."

"They ain't burnin none, is they?"

"Nosir."

"Well, be ticular, now. Don't you-all mess round the stack lumber. Stay bout the sawdust."

"Yessir."

"Yessir, Papa," Daniel said.

The boys turned and dashed toward the front door, crying out at each other as they ran.

"Cooter!" Louella shouted.

The sound of running feet ceased abruptly and for a moment the house was silent.

"Cooter, you draw me some water fo you go."

"Aw, Mama. Lettie get you some."

"I been drawin water all mornin long, boy," Lettie said. "Sides that, I got to feed her her dinner."

"Ain't going hurt you get that water," Louella said.

"Mama, I get you some when us———"

70

"Get Mama the water, Cooter," Albert said. "You going have a long time to play in the sawdust."

"Yessir," Cooter said, and returned to the kitchen to get the water bucket. ,

After the boys had gone Louella stacked the tin plates on the end of the table. "I got to get on up yonder. Get up there and do Miss Maureen washin."

"You going be by the sto?"

"I go by there when I finish."

"She out of her snuff. Better get her another jar."

"Is Mister Mathis chargin us the furnish now?"

"He chargin. Me and Mister Tittle seen him last week. He going furnish us like he been doing."

"I get her some, then."

Albert went out into the yard where he paused, thinking, then went on past the woodpile toward the creek and to the fields beyond. He thought of Preacher Tom's words as he walked, weighing them this way and that, but he could not bring himself to believe that anyone would mind his painting his house, even if they understood all that it meant to him.

"Folks like to see a man do the best he can," he said aloud, and he lifted his head and began to whistle.

He was ready to turn homeward when a sound suddenly stopped him in his tracks. He listened. It was the call of the first whippoorwill of spring. The call came strong and clear and it made his heart beat faster. He smiled and nodded to himself. Soon he would enter the fields to cut the earth into long dark rows for the cotton. The thought of the earth-smell of new furrows made him quicken with more excitement still, but he did not hurry. He walked slowly, looking at the old rows and naming to himself the plowpoints he must take to be sharpened at the blacksmith's shop.

FIVE

ALBERT STOOD at the edge of the field and watched Cooter run the turning plow up and down the long rows. Albert had broken the land the day before with the scooter stock, and now the new-turned earth fell across the field like dark ribbons, and behind the plow quick birds darted about in search of worms. It was the first year Cooter had helped to break the land and his rows were often crooked. Twice already Albert had plowed along with the boy, straightening the rows and showing his son how to handle the mule. Now, as Cooter came toward him, Albert smiled to himself. His son was breathing hard and sweat ran off the high forehead and onto the sides of his cheeks.

"You ain't tired, is you?"

"Nosir, Papa. Ain't me tired." He paused to catch

73

his breath. "Ain't me. It Mac gettin tired. Mac don't think he ever been plowed like this befo."

Mac rolled his big eyes around in their sockets. He looked at Cooter sadly, then shifted his eyes to Albert.

"I don't reckon Mac do," Albert said. "And I spec he do be a little tired."

Mac turned his head away from them both, as though hurt, and began to eat grass.

"Yessir," Cooter said. He turned and looked behind him. The row he had just finished was as crooked as a stick. "This one straight, ain't it, Papa?"

"It a good row, Cooter. Out there in the middle it bend a little, but we straighten that out. We got to have us some good rows this year, so's we can make that cotton really jump."

Cooter's face grew serious and a little sad and he looked at Albert a moment before he said, "Papa, how long it gonna take that mule learn to do the way he s'pose to do?"

At these words Mac jerked his head up, throwing his collar back against his shoulders, and stood with his head cocked a little to one side, as though listening.

"Ain't going take long," Albert said. "They say

when you plow a straight row you be's a man then. Say it take a man to plow a straight row. Ain't going take Mac long fo he know."

"I sho wish he hurry."

Mac shook his head and began to graze again.

Just now the foliage of the bushes behind Albert parted and Daniel came running out. The boy smelled of pine needles and there was dirt in his hair. He looked at Cooter beside the plow and came on over to Albert. "Can I plow the mule, Papa?"

"You can't plow no mule, Daniel," Cooter said. "You ain't big enough to plow no mule."

"You ain't neither, Cooter."

"I is, too. Ain't I, Papa?"

"Sho you is, Cooter-boy."

Albert looked at Cooter and recalled days when he had been fourteen, that time when he was not a boy any more nor yet a man. He was glad he could still remember and he smiled as he went to the plow.

"Come on help me, Daniel, while Cooter rest."

Daniel held the plow lines and sometimes the handles of the plow, but he soon tired and fell behind Albert. For a time he followed in the wake of the plow to dig his bare feet into the cool, firm dirt. Later he went to join Cooter beneath a tree. Albert plowed on and it was near midafternoon when he saw Louella cross the creek and come into the field. She walked quickly and carried a brown jug of water pressed against her side.

"I brung you some water."

"I sho thirsty for some, Mama."

The water gurgled as he drank and a small stream of it ran across his chin. He wiped his mouth on his jumper sleeve. "You done early, ain't you? I thought you yet up yonder."

"I ain't gone up there today." She put the corncob stopper back into the jug and glanced over the field. "I sunt Sistah up there to tell Miss Maureen I can't wash for her no mo."

"You ain't going do her washin no mo?"

"I sunt her word I ain't. She ain't paid me money for that washin going on six week. Been payin me with them old dresses she can't wear no mo. Sistah come back sayin Miss Maureen say come on up there anyways. Say her washin need doing. I sunt Sistah back, and Miss Maureen say I better come on, I know what good for me."

"You been ask her for the money, ain't you, Mama?"

76

"I ask her for it every time. But she say she ain't got it. And them old dresses wo out, and don't fit me noways. Don't fit Sistah neither, not even her. Miss Maureen got the money, would she give me it."

"She must is," Albert said. "I know Mister Dauber got money, way he been hauled all them logs back there in the winter."

"They got the money. They sho got the money. But then she say she can't pay for her washin."

"Sho help us out some, would she pay you."

"It would. But she won't. And then after Sistah come back the last time, Miss Maureen drove down to the house. Brought that big car right down the lane and ask me why I ain't come on. I told her and she say I ought to be proud to have them dresses. Say I ought to be proud to have them old dresses for doing her washin. I told her the dresses too big for me, and that made her madder yet. She say I ain't doing nothin noways but sittin on the porch all day. And I told her the dresses don't fit Sistah neither, not even her. And Miss Maureen ain't even got out the car, but stuck herself out the window and say why don't I use my head and cut the dresses down. And then back in the house I heard a moan and I told Miss

77

Maureen us need the money mighty bad. Then Miss Maureen just start that car up, out sayin no mo, and shot up the lane in a cloud of dust. So I brung you some water."

"Don't take you long do the washin, do it, Mama?"

"Take me long? It take me all e'nin. Miss Maureen act like I just made to do her work. Why I ought to work my fingers to the bone for nothin? Just tell me that, if'n you can. I just done come to think her washin mo'n I can do."

Albert looked at her. "It sho do be a heap to do. But if'n we going be ready in the fall when we sell the cotton, we going all need stay mighty busy."

"Ain't no use you talkin on," Louella said, and she rubbed the palm of her hand back and forth across her hip. "You know well as me how them folks is, and how they do."

She did not look at him and he studied her face until Cooter and Daniel came toward them.

"He ain't yet," Cooter was saying. "He know soon, but he don't know yet."

"Yes, he do, Cooter."

"No, he don't."

"Papa say he do," Daniel said.

"Papa ain't said that. He say it won't take him long."

"Papa know."

"Boy, you don't know what you talkin bout. You ask Papa."

"Papa? Don't that mule know how to walk the rows? Cooter say he don't."

"He learnin fast, I reckon," Albert said, still watching Louella's face. "You-all want some water?"

"You chillun been on that creek?" Louella said.

"No'm," Cooter said, drinking from the jug. "We been here helpin Papa."

"You better get on to that house and tote me some wood in. Ain't been a stick in that box all day."

Cooter handed the jug to Daniel and looked at his father, but Albert did not say anything, and Cooter said, "Yes'm. We get it, Mama."

"I ain't gonna go!" Daniel said, and dropped the jug. Water splashed across his feet.

"Yes, you is," Louella said. "And look what you doing! You get on there with Cooter fo I get me a switch."

Daniel giggled like a girl and skipped off across the rows calling to Cooter.

"Sometime them chillun try my nerves," Louella said. "If'n they ain't on that creek, they over here in the field."

"Them boys have them a time. And it going make me proud for them when the fall come. Till then, we going need work, Mama. Don't you reckon you can keep on going up yonder till fall? I know Miss Maureen give you the money if'n you won't take the dresses."

"I don't reckon I going no mo."

"You ought to go, Mama. It help us out."

Her eyes grew bright and her voice filled with anger. "Help us out! It help us out, all right. Seem like you want me just be work plum out. Well, you just go on hopin I go. Just hope on."

She jerked up the jug without looking at him and dashed off toward the creek.

He stood looking after her, wanting to call to her, to tell her it did not matter about the washing. But something kept him silent. When she was out of sight he turned back to the plow.

But the joy was gone from his work. After he plowed two rows he left the mule and went to the little opening to stand beside the pine tree. Though the day was quiet and the shade was cool, he did not feel the old comfort now. He wondered if it had been wrong for him to speak to Louella as he had. He hated, more than anything, to see her angry. The more he thought the more convinced he became that he had no right to expect her to do work except her own about the house. He began to feel so guilty that he hitched the mule to the slide, leaving the plow idle, and hurried home to talk to her.

Daniel said she had gone up the road. Albert led the mule up the lane and left him, harnessed, at the barn. Then he walked on past the crape-myrtle trees, in a small bare path that skirted the front of Mister Tittle's house. Miss Mary stood in the front yard shaking dust from a broom, but she did not look up and he went on out to the road. Beside the road, along the marshy edges of the sloughs, the May-haw trees were blooming and their pink flowers scented the air. But Albert hardly noticed their odor today. He searched the road, but saw only Augustus Brann, who had come out from the sawmill yard to head him off.

Augustus was the second son of Jenny Brann. He had been away to war, and fought, and come back to Longfield with a bullet wound in his leg. He limped a little when he walked, and worked for Mister Dillard. And he came to Albert's often, to visit Lettie.

"I hear some bad news, Prince." Augustus frowned.

Some people said Augustus resembled Albert, though Albert had never been able himself to tell. But he liked Augustus, liked the square set of his shoulders, the frank quiet strength of his eyes.

Albert stopped. "Somethin happen, Augustus?"

"It did, Prince. I hear them say at the mill a man was down bout dead over yonder."

"Aw, now. Who is it?"

"They say a mule got a tall man down," Augustus went on, shaking his head. "Say the mule got the man right down in the dirt and stomp him, then commence draggin the man crossways the field, back and forth."

Albert started to smile, but caught himself. "I sho ain't seen nobody, Augustus. Though I did hear a hollerin this mornin, and they was a man over there. But this man was bouncin a mule up and down like a rubber ball. They was so much sweat flyin it look like a good rain, and they ain't been a cloud in sight."

"I don't know, Prince. But they say the man just ain't had a chance."

"That a mule name of Mac, Augustus?"

"Hey, now!" Augustus laughed and slapped his leg. "Hey, now!"

"E'nin, Augustus."

"E'nin, Prince. You lookin like you been in that creek."

"Me and that mule been wadin a bit. You been busy?"

"Not none, Prince. They just ain't much doin round here when the mill shut down. This place seem duller than it been fo the war. And then when I ain't workin it be's worser yet."

"The mill look mighty dead," Albert said. He glanced up the road. "Augustus, is you seen——"

"Ain't nobody to cut logs," Augustus said. "Mister Dauber ain't hauled none this last week. Happen a little like this ever year, but since I come back here it get worser and worser. You know, Prince, they some folks ain't come back here after the war. And they some keep movin off. Ain't the same like it been fo the war."

"Sho ain't the same, Augustus."

"Now they say they going start that mill turnin on a Monday. But they don't know for sho. Just ain't gettin no logs."

"Folks in the field."

"I guess they is. Folks can make mo money cuttin logs, but when it time to make a crop they go in them fields. Go on in them fields when they know they ain't going make a dime."

"They do, Augustus."

Augustus shook his head. "Uncle Scott over there, so old he can't do nothin. But he out there in that little patch of his'n, out there with a hoe and rake, tryin dig that ground. And the muda grass strong and him weak."

"I guess it somethin make them do it," Albert said.

"I guess they is, Prince. How yo work comin?"

"Right well, Augustus."

"They say it going be a good year."

"I hopin it be's. I going be needin me a good piece of money this fall."

"You ain't bout to move off, Prince?"

"Not that, Augustus. Just fix things up some. I wonder is you seen Mama passin by?"

"I seen Louella going to'ad the sto. But it Lettie I been lookin for and ain't found. Just no tellin where she is. Look to me like I going have to marry that girl, keep her from runnin round so."

"You have to speak with her," Albert said, and turned to leave.

But Augustus grabbed him by the arm. "Looka here, Prince. Looka here. I done did that. I told that girl four-five time let's get married. But she ain't settle down to say yes or no. Stay in that car with Preacher Tom half the time, and keep puttin me off, way girls do. But I going get her, she don't watch out. You tell her I be over there tonight. And tell her don't go runnin off nowheres."

"I tell her," Albert said over his shoulder. "I sho tell her." And he left Augustus standing in the middle of the road and walked on to the store.

But he did not find Louella anywhere. He sat on the concrete step of the store porch, and he realized that he felt more tired than he had in weeks. He let his eyes close and did not open them until Mister Dauber drove up in his truck.

"E'nin, Mister Dauber."

"Good evening, Albert."

Albert went out to the truck. "Mister Dauber, is you seen Mama down to yo house?"

While he asked the question, Albert searched the other's eyes, which were like two circles of blue sky cut out and stuck into the deep-tanned face. The blue and the white of Mister Dauber's eyes were clean and clear and always reminded Albert of clothes scrubbed in a washtub and hung out to dry.

"Haven't been home since morning. But I guess she's down there, doing the washing. When're you going to lay by this year?"

"Hard to tell right now, Mister Dauber. But it likely be the middle of July."

"Some logs to cut when you're ready."

"Yessir. Soon's I lay by I going want to cut."

"Let me know," Mister Dauber said, springing off the truck. "You can cut when you're ready."

"I sho let you know."

Albert went back down the road. Ahead of him, along the horizon, dark clouds were forming and he heard a distant rumble of thunder. He hurried on, looking to right and left as he went, but he had reached Mister Tittle's barn before he saw Louella coming down the railroad track. He waited beside the barn gate, and when she drew near he said, "You going home, Mama?"

"Where it look like I going?" She did not change her pace, or look at him.

"I been lookin for you. To tell you I——"

"Don't say nothin to me. Not nothin!" She walked on past.

"Mama?"

Footsteps sounded behind him. It was Mister Tittle, with a sack in his hand.

"What's the matter with her?"

"Nothin. Nothin, Mister Tittle. It look like it comin a rain."

"I wanted that corn shelled today. We've got to get that bottom piece planted while it's dry."

"Yessir. I start on it now. I going start it now." He climbed into the corncrib, which was cool and dark and smelled of hay, and began to shuck the corn. Mister Tittle stood at the crib door.

"How much does that calf of yours weigh now?"

Albert did not look up. "He near a hundred, I reckon, Mister Tittle. He movin right on."

"My God, he ought to be!"

"Sir?"

"I say he ought to be moving on."

"Yessir. He growin fast."

"I was just telling Miss Mary this morning that Old Bertha was getting old."

"She ain't old, Mister Tittle."

"The cow could be old as Methuselah, as far as

Miss Mary knows. She at least knows Old Bertha's name. I sort of told her the cow was ten years old."

"Nosir. Old Bertha ain't near that old. You member her first calf just come here bout four year ago."

"Well, goddamn, Prince!" Mister Tittle slapped the wall of the crib with the sack. "Don't sit there and tell me how old the cow is. I said Miss Mary thinks she's that old. And not giving butter like she used to."

Albert looked at Mister Tittle, then looked down at the ear of corn he held, and nodded. "Yessir. Yessir. Miss Mary bout right. Old Bertha sho not givin much rich milk like she have did."

Mister Tittle paused, head and shoulders framed by the crib door. "That's right." And then: "It's going to be a good time for cotton planting next week. We'll be ready, won't we?"

"Yessir. I have the land ready."

Mister Tittle moved away. For a while Albert heard him walking about in the stalls. Then the chain rattled on the gate and Mister Tittle went back toward the house humming a little tune.

Though Albert hurried with the corn shelling, it was dark when he returned to the tenant house. Louella he found in the kitchen, busy and silent about the stove, and he saw the round dark spot where her dress stuck to the dampness on her back.

"You-all sit down," she said.

Albert wanted to talk with her but decided to wait until they were alone. He sat at the table with Cooter and Daniel and watched her put their supper on the table. When she had finished this task she went to sit on the wood in the stovewood box.

"Ain't you going eat, Mama?"

"You-all go on."

"Can I have me a calf next year, Papa?" Cooter said.

"Ain't you hungry?" Albert said.

"A calf the last thing in this world you need," Lettie said.

Louella did not answer him.

"Papa say he gonna get us a dog," Daniel said.

"Now that somethin you needin," Lettie said. "Way you-all hunts."

Albert did not see anger on Louella's face, but there was a tightness about her mouth, and he felt as though she sat scolding him. She worked too hard, he thought, and he told himself he must see that the boys, and Lettie, helped her more.

After supper, when they were alone in the

kitchen, he went over to the stove. "I help you with the dishes."

"I don't need no help."

But he took the plates anyway, drying them with care and stacking them on the back of the stove. Now that he had his chance to speak he waited, and all the dishes were dried before he said, "You ain't been up yonder, is you?"

"Up yonder where? I been to see Tilda. Her little girl mighty sick."

"I glad you ain't going do the washin."

"You sho change yo mind quick. This e'nin you been at me to go. Tellin me go on, when I got all my work to do."

"I don't want you go no mo, Mama."

She threw the dishwater out the back door and the tightness left her mouth. "I reckon I could go up there tomorrow."

"I ruther you don't go."

She wiped out the dishpan and hung it on a nail against the wall before she said, "You don't want me to, I won't go, then."

He had taken the dishcloth from her hand and spread it on the stove when the low moan began in the bedroom. He stood quietly, listening to the old woman's wail grow louder and louder, filling the house with its sound. Daniel ran crying into the kitchen and clutched at Albert's legs.

"She get worser all the time," Louella said, and hugged Daniel to her side.

In front of Albert the darkness pressed at the door, then came on into the kitchen a distance before it melted away in face of lamplight that shone dim as December moonlight. Outside, a restless bird set up a commotion among the leaves of the sweet-gum tree, squawking in that fussy, clear and lonely way birds have at night. And over on the road Minnie Sue's voice lifted calling, but got no answer.

"She do," Albert said, and thought they had better go on in to her.

SIX

THE COTTON CAME UP, spring passed quickly as always, and soon the long hot days of summer had come. Mister Tittle came to the fields every day, sometimes working beside Albert, sometimes not. Mister Tittle never talked about the house, but the time had come when Albert needed advice. He waited to speak, until one day the right moment came.

"They say this going be a good year, Mister Tittle."

"They say, Prince. They say it is. But they say everything under God Almighty's sun at one time or another. But maybe it will. Can't say yet. I need it to be. And you do too, if you go ahead with that house."

"How much paint you figure I going need?"

Mister Tittle crumbled a lump of dirt in his hand

and let the soil sift through his fingers a long time before he answered. "I don't know. I'm going to leave all that up to you, like I said. Do you know how to add?"

"Yessir."

"Do you know how to multiply?"

"Nosir."

"Well, goddamn. I guess you'd better estimate."

June came. The air was clear and often, high overhead, flights of blackbirds moved like dark leaves across the sky. One afternoon as Albert went home with a bundle of young cornstalks on the slide for the calf he saw Augustus standing beside the pasture. An idea came to Albert and he hurried the mule along.

Augustus stood with his hands deep in his pockets. His shoulders drooped, his face was long and he looked as though he was about to cry. "I been waitin see you, Prince," he said. "Wantin talk with you."

"Who yo trouble is, Augustus?"

"Lettie, Prince. You know how she do's, and I been wantin her settle down with me. But I can't get her say nothin. I come over here this mornin. And then in a little while Preacher Tom he come too. And she got in the car with him and just rid off."

Augustus paused a moment and studied the ground. "Say she going help him sell them banilla epstracts. I can't make no sense from the way she do. And I been thinkin you may would talk with her."

"I don't know if it do no good, Augustus. Lettie strongheaded when she want to be. But I sho try. To see can I get her make up her mind."

"I be much-oblige if you do it."

"I talk with her. You going be back by the house this e'nin?"

"I s'posin so."

"I going need yo help with somethin bout Sadday. We talk bout it this e'nin."

"I be back, Prince."

When Albert neared home he saw Daniel jump off the back steps and run across the yard.

"You comin home, Papa?"

"I comin, Daniel."

"I sho glad."

Daniel took one of Albert's fingers into his hand and trotted along beside him. "Papa, what Mac real name is?"

Mac, hearing his name called, pointed his ears.

"He just Mac. He don't have no name cep that."

"He big, ain't he?"

"He pretty big."

"Do he know I talkin bout him, Papa?"

"I spec he do. Mac smarter'n he look."

Mac lifted his head high, as though he thought himself a horse and would prance a bit.

Albert stopped the slide in the shade of the sweet-gum tree. Beneath the tree old gum balls lay over the ground and Daniel stood looking at these with a brightness in his eyes.

Albert brushed dirt from Daniel's head. "You been diggin in this yard?"

Daniel dropped onto his knees and began to collect the gum balls, as though some great plan had come into his head.

"What you going do, now?"

"Nothin, Papa."

Albert smiled to himself. "You sho you ain't?"

"Yessir."

"All right, then."

As Albert went toward the kitchen Daniel began to rush about the yard to drop one of the gum balls into each of the holes he had dug in the yard with a spoon. Albert shook his head and went inside.

Lettie and Louella, in the bedroom barefooted, wearing loose summer dresses, were struggling with the old woman, trying to give her green medicine from a bottle. The old woman sat wrapped in two sweaters and a shawl, which they had not been able to get her to take off, and she fought at Lettie and Louella with her hands.

"Don't you hurt her," Albert said.

"She got to take this stuff," Louella said.

While Louella poured half the bottle of liquid into her mouth the old woman did not move or moan or make any sound. But a moment later she spat a long thin stream of liquid across the floor. The medicine made a dark streak across the boards at Albert's feet.

"Now, look at that," Louella said. "Just look at that! I don't know what we going do with her."

"I s'pose it best just leave her lone."

Louella went muttering off to the kitchen and Albert sat in a chair opposite Lettie. He did not know how to begin to talk to her; he drummed his fingers against the bottom of the chair, thinking.

He was almost ready to speak when Lettie said, "You seen Augustus?"

"I seen him there by the pastah."

"He actin worrified. Like he sick."

"I don't guess Augustus sick. But he sho like you a heap."

Lettie giggled. "He say he do."

"Augustus be mighty glad if'n you would marry him. Augustus a good boy, for somebody."

Lettie stretched her leg far out and moved her bare toe back and forth over a crack in the floor. "He all right, I reckon. But then Augustus ain't got no car."

Albert looked at her, watched her move her toe back and forth, and sat at a loss for words. Then he remembered his promise to Augustus. "I know it fine to ride in the car. But Augustus mo yo age. Jenny gettin old, too . . ."

"Papa!" Daniel called from the yard.

". . . and Augustus going need him a wife. Don't seem to me like you ought to keep Augustus the way he is. Lessen you serious."

"I can't help the way he feel."

"But you can make up yo mind bout him."

"Hooooo!" Daniel shouted.

"And don't be just teasin him on like you do's."

He expected Lettie to become angry, but she hung her head. "I don't know what I going say."

Louella ran across the kitchen floor.

"That be's up to you."

"Stop him!" Louella cried. "Stop him, Daniel!"

Albert stood, and went on quickly. "This e'nin be

97

a good time to talk with Augustus. He say he comin back bout nighttime."

Louella rushed into the room. "You better go yonder. Quick! That mule going in the garden! Going right in that garden!"

Albert started running. As he went out the door he heard Lettie say, "Preacher Tom say he comin, too."

Augustus returned first, and Albert walked with him out to the lot. They stood in the twilight with their arms resting on the lot fence, watching the calf eat the cornstalks for a while before Albert told Augustus about the house.

"You going do——"

"Going paint it white, Augustus."

Augustus looked off without saying anything, as though in his mind he put the pieces of a puzzle together. Silent moments passed before his face lighted up. "Naw, you ain't, now?"

"I is. Can I get the paint."

"What Mister Tittle going say to that?"

"He say go head with it. Say it up to me. And I wonder if you may can help me figure out the paint I going need? On a Sadday."

"I sho will, Prince. I be glad to help you. If Sadday come, I be here. Here helpin you figure."

The flicker of headlights appeared on the lane; the lights moved on down to the house, went out then, and they saw Preacher Tom get out of his car and go to sit on the porch.

"There he is," Augustus said. "Ain't good dark, and there he is. Ready, fo his Lawd, to sit all night."

"I done spoke with her," Albert said as he followed Augustus toward the house. "And you know how girls is. But she may going talk serious with you to-night."

Albert believed Lettie would. He hurried into the house, leaving Augustus on the porch with Lettie and Preacher Tom. "Mama?"

"I here on the back step."

"We going do it Sadday."

"Going do what Sadday?"

"Figure the paint. Augustus comin help me."

"You ain't got no money yet."

"But I needin know. I going sell that calf fo long, fo he eat up everythin on the place. Augustus say he comin help me."

"Augustus look like he needin help hisself, way he going bout with his face on the ground."

"I spoke with Lettie bout him."

"What Sistah say?"

"She ain't said much, neither this way nor that."

"Sistah got her ways. But then she just a girl."

"I believe she going make up her mind, though."

"This e'nin?"

"I spec her to."

"Let's go in yonder, then."

Louella went into the bedroom and drew a chair close against the wall and began listening for voices on the porch. Albert sat near her, opposite the old woman, and they waited in the hot summer darkness, but the only sound they heard came from over on the road, where trucks were passing.

"You reckon she going cide?" Louella whispered.

Albert nodded. "Just takin her time."

But when an hour passed and they still heard nothing from the porch, Albert's mind turned to thoughts of the house. He wondered if Louella knew how much he thought of it all. He could not tell but he sometimes noticed her being restless. He lighted the lamp quietly and sat studying her face, which she kept close to the wall. In the soft light she resembled Lettie and he remembered her as he had seen her that day when she had danced in a yellow dress. That had been a long time ago, he thought, and leaned near enough to her to see the thin lines, like dark threads, that had begun to form about her mouth. He suddenly wanted to touch her lips, to hold her against him and talk to her. He moved his arm toward her, but she leaned nearer the wall and they heard Lettie.

"Don't be too close to me, Augustus. You move back some."

"What she say?" Albert said.

"Tellin Augustus move off from her."

The night seemed to grow hotter and Albert removed his jumper. Opposite him the old woman was sweating hard and a sour odor came from her corner of the room.

"Listen," Louella said.

"You get back, Preacher Tom," Lettie said. "It be's hot. You move back there."

"Tellin Preacher Tom move back, too," Louella said.

Then Augustus spoke. "You have to get up mighty early, don't you, Preacher Tom? Sellin yo stuff."

"Amen, Augustus. Sometime I do."

Lettie laughed softly, and Louella pressed her head against the wall. But Preacher Tom made no move to go. Instead, he said, "They say they going start that mill tomorrow."

"Say they is?"

"It what they say. It mean mill folks be rollin out with that whistle, Augustus, way fo day."

"Now, they will."

But Augustus did not go.

Louella shook her head and sighed. "Sistah ain't going say nothin. It already going on ten o'clock."

"Look to me like she go on and say somethin," Albert said.

He and Louella went to bed and even after the midnight roosters began to crow Albert still heard the low voices mumbling there on the porch.

SEVEN

Augustus had told his mother that on Saturday he would help Albert estimate the paint needed for the tenant house. Jenny had dropped the overalls she patched and a moment later she was picking her way along a little path to tell R-Rula and Minnie Sue. Minnie Sue had been up before daybreak next morning to tell Dora and Solo Thompson, and R-Rula had hurried to the road to wave down Pearl, who later told A.C. By midafternoon that day the news moved about Longfield like willow fuzz, flying here, pausing, lifting onward again, swirling about among musical voices, low intent voices which said:

"Prince Albert going paint his house white."

"What that you say?"

"Prince going paint his house white."

"His house white?"

"They say he is."

"You don't mean it?"

"They say it. Say he been plannin on it a long
time. Say he going figure the paint on Sadday."

"Aw, now. Aw."

"It what they say. R-Rula seen Jenny last night
and Jenny say Prince Albert done ask Augustus to
help figure it out."

"I do say. I do say."

"Going figure it on Sadday."

"I do say."

A little silence and a shake of the head. "I got to
get on to the sto."

"E'nin."

A pause, a question: "Sadday, you say?"

"It what they say."

They passed the news on, repeating it in soft, solemn voices. Old heads leaned forward in a strain,
hearing, then nodded slowly and thoughtfully re-
clined again. Young faces grew still and awed for
one reflective moment, then broke into soft stares
of wonder. As the news went round and round and
their voices together made a chant of it they began to
feel as though something very deep was about to
touch their lives. They did not know whether to
laugh or to pray, so they remained content to spread

the news on, now in questions, now in whispers, always in splendid low musical voices. By Saturday morning everyone in Longfield knew, and they all waited for the noon whistle at the sawmill.

When the sound began they all paused to listen. The long-throated call of the whistle carried far and a little mournfully over the land. When its voice died away beyond the pine trees they nodded their heads and left the road to walk across the pasture toward the tenant house. They walked in ones and twos, for none had expressed the intent to gather, yet all had understood.

Albert had known from Augustus how the news had spread, and twice he had overheard people talking about what he planned to do. He stood on the porch, watching the people who gathered on the road. But when the sound of the whistle began he went inside the house, and it was Louella, passing near the front door, who first spoke of the people who came across the pasture. "Look yonder at all them folks."

"You see Augustus yet?" Albert said.

Louella smoothed her hair with the palm of her hand and spoke over her shoulder into the dim quiet of the room. "It a heap of folks. Yonder R-Rula and

Solo. And down the lane come Pearl and Minnie Sue and Tilda with her little sick girl. Tilda know better'n have that girl out the bed. Yonder Jenny. And Monroe. But I don't see Augustus."

"He be on."

"Don't they know this a Sadday?"

She impatiently pressed her dress across her hip and frowned. "We going to the sto. We out us groceries, and got to go to the sto. Them folks know this a Sadday."

"Me and Augustus going do that figurin, Mama. I s'pose they want to see."

"I s'pose they do. And I s'pose they know we have to get on up to that sto."

"When we gonna go?" Cooter said.

"Folks a-comin, Cooter," Louella said. "You fix yo'self up. Yo shirttail out and yo ov'alls ain't hooked. Daniel? Daniel! Scrape that dirt from out yo head."

Daniel stood near the wall of the room with his eyes centered to a crack. People were already gathering in the yard. Big Sam, R-Rula's dog, turned round and round, as though chasing his tail, and lay in the shade of the peach tree.

"Ain't no dirt in my head, Mama."

"Yes, they is, Daniel," Albert said.

Daniel took his eye from the crack. "Where the dirt, Papa?"

"Right here," Albert said, brushing dirt from the boy's head. "You see it?"

Daniel grinned and leaned against Albert's leg.

"They always dirt in yo head," Louella said. "And you stay way from that crack. Folks be thinkin you ain't never seen nobody befo."

"When we gonna go to the sto?" Cooter asked.

"We go soon's them folks leave," Louella said. "But you fix yo'self up! I done told you twenty times fix yo'self!"

Albert went out to the porch. The murmur of voices in the yard stopped with the sound of his steps, and the people turned to look at him with wonder and admiration in their eyes. He was one of them, their neighbor, yet now they acted almost formal.

"E'nin, Aunt Rooney, and Jenny," Albert said. "E'nin, Uncle Scott. Monroe, Tilda and R-Rula. E'nin, you-all."

Augustus came up then and Albert joined him out beside the chimney.

"Augustus and Albert look like they brothers," someone said.

"Sho do," another agreed.

Albert saw the others who kept coming across the pasture. Among them came Aunt Molly Paterson, who lived alone on an old-age pension. She wore a black silk dress with a white lace collar, and above the collar she held her head rigid and erect and looked about with beady eyes. The dress she wore was one she had been saving to be buried in. Albert knew that she had never worn it before, and he guessed that during the morning, after long and painful thought, she had decided to come with the others and would appear only in the black dress which one day would bear her up to heaven. She stood on the fringe of a small group, but paid them no attention. Finally her eyes wandered to where Augustus and Albert stood beside the chimney.

Albert was ready to begin making the estimate. He gave Augustus a pencil and they walked around the house. From time to time Augustus wrote a figure on the wrinkled corner of a brown paper bag. The group of people who had gathered followed them closely, all except Jenny, who stood a little apart. It was her son Augustus, so recently returned from the war with a bullet wound in his leg, who had been called in to help make the estimate, and she acted as though she did not think it fitting that she should mingle with the others.

They all made three trips around the house before Augustus wrote down a final figure and stopped beside the peach tree near the water well.

"How much you figure it going take?" Albert said.

"The way I see it here, Prince, it going take three gallon."

Albert repeated this amount to himself. Then he studied Augustus' figures for a time before he looked thoughtfully up the lane. Jenny, still to one side, looked at Augustus with a question on her face. A moment later Albert fell into a discussion with Augustus and they went over the figures again.

"How much it going take?" Aunt Molly Paterson said. "You-all been had plenty time."

"We ain't got it yet," Augustus said.

Aunt Molly came forward, her old voice lifting. "Don't know yet? And been at them figures going on a hour?"

Those near her smiled at this outburst, and they exchanged little knowing glances as they moved back to let her pass.

"You boys been runnin round the house like a circle saw," Aunt Molly said. "And it time you knowed what it going take. Drop them figures, Augustus, and look at the house. Yo mama done teached you mo sense than this."

At these words Jenny trembled and nodded her head. "You right, Aunt Molly. You sho right."

"Look at the house," Aunt Molly said. "It got four sides, ain't it? Well, anybody know it going take bout one gallon for one side, and four time one make four. That be's four gallon. But Prince Albert going need him some extra for the high spots and a little mo for the low spots. That going mount to one gallon. Four and one make five, Augustus. But then that house mighty gray. Prince going need him two coat of paint to hide that mighty gray. Five and five make ten, Augustus, and you wastin yo time with them figures."

Albert smiled and nodded. "Aunt Molly bout right, Augustus. Ten gallon sho sound right."

"I s'pose she right," Augustus said. He crumpled the paper in his hand and looked at Aunt Molly, who stood archly with her beady eyes fastened on him. "I s'pose she right."

Jenny's face grew sad. She tucked her hands into the folds of her dress and turned away, walking slowly, with her head down, as though searching the pasture grass for some lost object.

"How much you-all say it going take?" Solo said.

"Ten gallon," Albert said. "It going take ten gallon."

Voices lifted, repeating the amount. The voices rose higher and higher, so that none of them heard the car on the lane and did not see it until it came to a sudden stop beside them.

Preacher Tom jumped from beneath the steering wheel and rushed forward beating the air with his arms.

"He want to see you, Prince. He say come up there. Say come right on. They up there talkin, sittin round they dominoes talkin. Standin round and talkin. And he say you come right on up there."

"Who say come up there?" Albert said.

"*He* say it."

"Speak clear, Preacher Tom," Aunt Molly said. "Cam yo'self and speak clear."

"It Mister Mathis! Up at the sto. He shoutin round with his head in a fit, and his hands in a fit. Them folks done heard what you aimin to do. And Mister Mathis say you beat it up to that sto. You know how that man can get rage-i-fied."

"Now, he can," someone said.

"They say he can," another replied.

Albert did not say anything, but stood quietly, looking at the ground.

"You going?" Louella said.

"I got to go up to the barn and feed that mule," Albert said.

For a time the people before him chatted quietly behind their hands in low voices. Then R-Rula and Monroe left. Soon Aunt Molly went too, and so they all began to disperse, moving away across the pasture in ones and twos, as they had gathered. They went out to the road and headed for the store, where Albert knew they would wait to see what he would finally do. He sat on the porch with his boys at his side.

"Ain't you going up there?" Louella said.

"I don't know." Daniel had drawn a hopscotch figure in the hard dirt at the foot of the steps, and Albert's thoughts leaped from square to square of the figure, and back again, without reaching any decision.

"You don't go, that man be down here."

"I don't know."

"Will you give me a nickel, Papa?" Daniel said. He climbed onto Albert's knee. "I wanna pop."

"I going on," Louella said.

"I be on, Mama."

"You chillun come on," Louella said.

"I gonna stay with Papa," Cooter said.

"I gonna stay, too," Daniel said.

"What you-all going stay for? He just going feed that mule."

"I going help him," Daniel said.

"Better go on with Mama, Daniel. I get up there, I buy you the pop."

"You get me the pop for sho, Papa?"

"I sho get you one, I get up there."

Daniel ran across the yard after Louella, who had walked on without looking back.

Inside the house the old woman began to moan. Her voice was high, not like it had ever been before. Albert and Cooter went into the bedroom.

"Listen, Papa. What make her start that now?"

Albert put his hand on her shoulder, trying to quiet her. And she quieted some, though her voice still held the strange quality that surprised him. She was trying to say something. He leaned near her and heard the words that came from her wrinkled lips.

"Death be's a little man, and he go from do' to do'. Death be's a little man, and he go from do' to do'. He be's a little . . ."

She motioned for him to come closer.

"But they mo," she whispered. "They mo you got to know."

She made a vague gesture with her hand and did not say any more.

Albert drew his hand away from her shoulder and stood looking down at her while he repeated her words over to himself. An odd sensation passed over him. "She funny," he said.

"Sho is, Papa. You reckon she hungry?"

"She likely is," Albert said, seizing this solid fact as something he understood and with which he could deal.

He hurried into the kitchen, but the only thing he could find for her to eat was a baked sweet potato left over from two days before. He peeled the potato and placed it in her withered hands. When he touched her the sensation came over him again and he felt that he must get out of the house at once. He wheeled toward the door. "Come on, Cooter. We got to feed that mule and get on up yonder."

EIGHT

THE AFTERNOON was hot as Albert and Cooter walked side by side along the road. Ahead of them a group of people sat waiting, in front of the store in the shade of the sweet-gum tree, where Old Reuben, who brewed bad liquor in the woods at night and on Saturdays came to Longfield to cut hair and sell his product, bent over the patient head of a customer who sat on a wooden block. Those near the block were suddenly quiet, and kept their eyes on Albert. Bottles of soda water grew warm unnoticed, and fingers failed to shell peanuts that had been bought from Aunt Maisie, who could always be found about the store on Saturday selling for a nickel cupfuls of roasted peanuts she took from a flour sack at her side.

"E'nin, Uncle Reuben," Albert said.

"E'nin, Prince Albert." Old Reuben pressed his gray head close against Albert's chest and whispered up to him. "I done heard the talkin. And I tell you what. Do you need anythin, I got a little bottle out there in the woods won't cost you nothin. Not a red cent."

"Much-oblige, Uncle Reuben. I don't guess I be needin none."

"Hey, Prince," A.C. called. "You get ready, I be glad to help you with yo paintin."

"E'nin, you-all," Albert said.

"E'nin, Prince Albert."

"E'nin, Prince."

"E'nin."

Albert walked among them, and their faces, which had been watchful in silent reposes, came to life in greeting. For a moment sunshine sifting through the leaves of the tree fell across Albert's face, and he smiled to himself, for he understood the words that none of them spoke to him. But when he glanced toward the store their faces assumed the gravity which he felt grow on his own. He lingered a moment more, standing very still, then turned away without a word.

"Papa," Daniel called. He ran across the gravel apron, packed hard as concrete, which skirted the front of the store. "You gonna get me the pop?"

"You hush bout that pop," Louella said, coming up behind him.

"Papa say he gonna———"

"You hush!" Louella banged her ragged purse down on Daniel's head. To Albert she said, "You be ticular how you talk to that man. You be careful what you say. You know he a man don't take nothin from folks."

"Don't you-all come in the sto," Albert said, and moved on.

"I wanna pop," Daniel said.

"I ain't going tell you no mo hush bout that pop!"

Albert was careful not to slam the screen door when he went into the store, where the air smelled of pickled pig feet and new leather harness, and a dim walled-in light gave a feeling of coolness. He let his eyes travel to the rear of the store, where he heard voices rise up as though from a cave. He did not go on back to the voices, but paused midway down the long aisle, beside a counter that held a long narrow showcase full of candies—hard lemon pieces, butter-fingers, peppermint sticks with their red and white stripes circling, green, red and orange gumdrops coated with fine sugar—and silver bells in a box.

Across the aisle from the candy case, on a table holding dishes and glassware, a black cat sat in a serving bowl. Beyond a stove that stood in the middle of the floor, around the cleared end of a square counter, Mister Jay and Mister Dauber and Mister Dillard and Mister McKinley sat with their hands over their dominoes. But Albert saw they were not playing at their game now but had half turned on their seats and were watching him.

Mister Roberts, who stood to one side, looked from Albert to the domino players and said, "It's this sort of thing puts my land idle."

The domino players made no reply and did not appear to notice that Mister Roberts turned and strode up the aisle to the door.

"E'nin, Mister Mathis," Albert said.

Mister Mathis dropped potatoes into a sack one by one, and after the front door slammed behind Mister Roberts the thump of potato against potato made the only sound in the store. As though urged into movement by the silence, the black cat stirred slowly, rose from out of the serving bowl and leaped lightly across the aisle to the counter at Albert's right. A covey of fat flies buzzed into the air and the cat began to nibble a round yellow cheese.

"Scat!" Mister Mathis cried. He grabbed a butcher's cleaver and lunged across the floor.

The cat leaped onto the floor and scampered toward the back door. A lean white dog jumped from under a counter and dashed off in chase.

Mister Mathis mopped at beads of moisture on his head as he went to a silver-coated cash register spotted with brown scars where the paint had flaked away. The little spots were the color of the birthmark on Mister Mathis' neck. The birthmark was as large as an egg, and it extended downward from the lobe of Mister Mathis' ear. The merchant scratched at his ear just now and Albert saw the diamond ring Mister Mathis wore on the little finger of his left hand. The diamond was the size of a pea, and Mister Mathis had a way of moving his hand that made the stone sparkle.

"E'nin, Mister Mathis."

A smile came to Mister Mathis' face. "Good evening, Albert."

Albert shifted his weight from one foot to the other and leaned lightly against the counter, while from the corner of his eye he saw the domino players stand, near the stove, to stare at him. He waited for Mister Mathis to say something more, but the store owner had turned to look up the aisle, where a square of warm sunlight came in and lay across the floor like a patch of yellow cloth.

"You want to see me, Mister Mathis?"

Mister Mathis looked at Albert as though he just remembered that the other stood across from him. "Damn hot weather's really here," he said, and went to a long red icebox to move his hand about in cold water. "What'd you like to drink, Albert? Strawberry, lemon or orange?"

"Sir?"

"Strawberry, lemon or orange?"

"Yessir."

"Strawberry?"

"Yessir."

Mister Mathis uncapped two bottles of strawberry soda and handed one to Albert. Albert looked at the men standing beside the stove, then back at Mister Mathis, and began to drink.

"Much-oblige, Mister Mathis."

"Be better with some cheese, wouldn't it?"

"Yessir, it sho would."

Mister Mathis took the butcher's cleaver from the counter and turned to the thick round cheese. He waved flies away with the hand which held the diamond ring and cut two big portions of the cheese. He placed these on a piece of brown wrapping paper with a handful of soda crackers he took from a tin box.

"Help yourself."

"Nosir. I s'pose——"

"Go ahead and eat it."

"Yessir." Albert began to eat.

"Good, ain't it?"

"Yessir, Mister Mathis."

"I know how you like cheese. You and Louella and your boys."

"Yessir. We love us cheese."

"You act pretty hungry."

Albert smiled. "Yessir. I been a little hungry."

"Look at that fool nigger eat," Mister Jay said.

Albert remembered that Mister Jay had at one time been constable. But he had fined everybody in sight for one thing or another and had not been elected to a second term.

"You'll want groceries today if you're that hungry," Mister Mathis said.

Albert did not know what to make of Mister Mathis' behavior; he studied the other's face. "We out, Mister Mathis. And needin some things."

"I hear you did some estimating this afternoon. Down at your house on John Tittle's place."

"Yessir. Yessir, we did. Mister Tittle say I can paint that house, can I get the paint. And I been plannin. I got hold of me a calf from Mister Walker that I going sell fo long. With the money he bring and what I has from the crop, I hopin to get the paint."

Mister Mathis' face did not change. "That'll be the first white nigger's house in this county. You know that?"

"Mister Tittle say it will."

"It will," Mister Mathis said. His lower lip dropped. "If you get it painted. You want your groceries now?"

"Yessir. I go head and get them now."

Albert followed Mister Mathis to a small wooden bin and looked at a side of lean salt meat which Mister Mathis placed on the counter.

"Good meat," Mister Mathis said. "How much are you going to need?"

"We going need bout ten pound, Mister Mathis."

The store owner placed the blade of a sharp knife along the briny edge of the meat. "About this much?"

"A good bit mo'n that, Mister Mathis. Bout ten pound."

"Maybe this'll last you for a while." Mister Mathis moved the knife back and quickly cut a piece of meat not half an inch thick. "I don't get this good meat often." He threw the thin cut of meat onto the scales. "That's a full pound."

"That won't hardly last us——"

"Anything else?" Mister Mathis asked, and a faint smile came to his lips.

"A sack of flour, and some sugar, and a can of lard——"

"You've got a pound of meat. And that's all you get. You understand that?"

"Nosir, I——"

"I'm cutting your credit off. Every cent of it! You can understand that, I guess?"

"I makin that crop, Mister Mathis. And them chillun——"

"You don't get another goddamn cent till you come to your senses. You'll change your mind about some things when you get hungry. Now get out."

Albert stood rooted to the floor, unable to bring himself to move.

"I said get out!"

Albert turned slowly. As he walked up the aisle he saw a queer smile pull at the corners of the little merchant's mouth. Some laughter came from the men around the stove.

"That cheese'll be on your account," Mister Mathis shouted.

But Albert was already out the door. He did not look to right or left, but he felt a hundred solemn eyes searching his own when he crossed the gravel apron and stepped onto the dusty road. To his right the sun was the color of a carrot, and against the late-afternoon sky the foliage of the sweet-gum tree loomed up like a dark cloud rushing down at him.

"Papa!" Daniel cried. "Where my pop?"

Albert paused an instant. Behind him, close at his heels, he heard the patter of his son's approaching steps. He stared down at the road and walked on.

"Papa!"

Albert's steps quickened. He walked faster, and faster again. Then he began to run, and his feet splattered quick clouds of dust into the air.

NINE

ALBERT DID NOT STOP running until he reached the tenant house. Now he sat in the bedroom. Before him the old woman slumped in her chair in the corner; he noticed that her body gave off a peculiar smell. He looked at her, but did not see her clearly. His shoulders dropped and he did not try to lift them. A wasp buzzed through the open shutter, paused above his head and darted out again. His head bent forward and there came into view a pattern of grain marks in the boards at his feet. Like the grain marks, his mind did not go in a straight line or make a circle. His thoughts eddied about in his head like driftwood at the edge of a current, waiting to be stirred free and drawn into the moving stream. A stillness as of deep water held him.

Once, when he looked up, he saw that the old woman's head had tilted far back, as though she strained for breath. But it did not occur to him to move her into a more comfortable position. He sat on and on, with a matchstick hanging unused in the corner of his mouth. When the sun went down and deep shadows slipped over the room the tinkling of Old Bertha's bell came from the lane. This familiar sound surprised Albert. He thought with a start that he had to go milk and to feed Mac. Then he recalled that he had fed the mule already, and Mister Tittle always milked on Saturdays. Albert's mind began to move better now and he lifted his head.

A full moon had come up before he heard voices on the lane. The voices grew clear and he listened.

"What been wrong with Myrabell, Sistah?"

"I don't know. She told Pearl she feel like she wantin to faint."

"That a new dress Pearl had on?"

"Pearl say the dress come from New Awleans. But she ain't foolin nobody. That dress just home-made."

"Where she get it?"

"Right there from Mister Mathis. And had Minnie Sue make it up for her. Minnie Sue told me. But Pearl up there swishin bout like she somebody on a visit."

"Give me that stick," Cooter said.

"This my stick, Cooter," Daniel said. "I scarin snakes off."

"Give me it, now."

"You chillun hush," Louella said. "You been tryin on my nerves all day. It time you-all hush that fuss."

"You come here side of me, Cooter," Lettie said. "Let Daniel keep the stick. Me and you don't care do he have the old stick."

"Mama, make Lettie leave me lone."

"I going take the stick to you, you don't hush that fuss. Sistah ain't botherin you."

"I scarin snakes," Daniel said. "I got a stick in my hand and I scarin snakes."

There was a silence and Albert heard their footsteps on the pasture. He began to think of what he must say to them.

"What Prince told Mister Mathis, Sistah?"

"They ain't no tellin. You seen him well as me. Runnin off down that road like he done, out sayin nothin. And he know well and good we needin us grocery."

"Augustus say he heard Mister Mathis say he go-

127

ing to the county seat first thing Monday mornin. Mister Mathis say he going down there to see the chantry clerk."

"They sho somethin going on."

Their feet sounded on the loose boards of the porch. Albert took the matchstick from his mouth.

"Papa?"

"Here I is, Daniel."

"You ain't bought me the pop, Papa."

"You hush up bout that," Louella said. She came into the room where Albert sat. "Why you sittin in the dark? We needin a light."

"They ain't much oil in the lamp. It best we don't use it up."

"Them folks up yonder all talkin bout you runnin. They say they ain't never seen no man with his face like yo's, comin off from that sto. What Mister Mathis done?"

"I told him bout the house. He ain't like it, and he cut us credit off. He know what things mean to me, mo'n just paintin the house. And he cut us credit off."

"In the middle of yo crop?"

"He charge me one pound of meat and say I ain't going get nothin mo. Say see can I come to my senses with a pound of meat. So we going do out his credit."

"You go see Mister Tittle?"

"I ain't been up there. I ain't going go runnin up to him."

"I sho like to know how you think we going get by, out nothin t'eat."

"We have some corn, and them collards."

"Bugs already at them collards."

He felt as though he had failed her and he wished she would say something to help drive his own doubts away.

"You full of pride," she said. "I know the house mean a heap. But do it mean mo'n somethin t'eat?"

"We have somethin. And we just go on with things by usself."

"Look to me like we been going on by usself too long now."

"A man have to pay for things. Have to pay, and then pay some mo."

Her voice grew sad. "We been payin. We been here fifteen year payin. But I ain't seen nothin we bought. Not nothin. That Sunday dress of mine seven year old, and failin at the seams."

He searched her face. "I mean mo'n that, Mama. A man pay for things that move bout inside him."

"You proud," she said. "You just proud."

"You ain't even got us no cheese, Papa," Daniel said.

"It time you be's in bed, Daniel."

"Nosir, it ain't, Papa. I hungry."

"Augustus heard Mister Mathis say he going to the county seat Monday mornin. First thing, to see the chantry clerk."

"See him bout what?"

"He ain't told nobody."

"It ain't nothin bout this e'nin. It sho can't be nothin bout that."

Albert lifted Daniel and took him to the other bedroom and put him to bed. "You go sleep, now."

"Papa, you ain't hug my neck."

Albert hugged his son and returned to the other room.

"Tell Cooter come on, Papa," Daniel said. "It dark in here."

"You better go yonder with him, Cooter. You know he can't never sleep till you go to bed."

"I don't know what we going do," Louella said, as though to herself. She crossed the room to the old woman. "And here she sit. Better off than we is, I reckon. Don't know nothin and ain't doing nothin. Just sittin like she do."

Louella's eyes suddenly grew round. She leaned toward the old woman. "What her head doing sittin like this?"

A vague memory stirred inside Albert, like a night dream not quite recalled by day. But he did not answer.

"She all right, Sistah?"

They gathered around the old woman to look, but the bad odor that came from her made them move back a step. Cooter tiptoed to the door and peered into the room. Daniel came up behind his brother and stood naked, rubbing his eyes. Outside a cloud drifted past, moving its slow shadow over the earth. And far away down the railroad track a screech owl sent his cry into the night.

"You better put her in her bed," Louella said.

The old woman was heavier than Albert remembered and when she did not move he bent down to look into her eyes. They were half opened and filled with moonlight. He placed his fingers on her wrist and thought of the words she had spoken to him earlier, in the afternoon. He straightened up and let out

131

a deep breath. But for a moment more he looked down at her. Her half-closed eyes appeared to be staring at him. He looked across the room.

"What the matter?" Louella said.

"She dead, Mama."

"She dead." Louella's voice filled with fright. "She ain't dead?" She spoke in that unbelieving way relatives have when first hearing of death; when, afraid, they speak half statement, half question, wanting to be deceived. Albert had heard it before—from his father when his mother died. "She ain't dead?"

"She is."

Cooter and Daniel ran into the room.

Albert pulled a quilt over the old woman's head and crossed the room to Louella and they all hung against one another beside the shutter where the moonlight shone in.

"She been a good old woman," Lettie said.

"She sho have suffer her time."

"She sho did that."

They all paused silent for a time, until presently Albert said, "I have to let the burial know. I have to let them know tonight."

He would need to use a telephone and the only one in Longfield belonged to Mister Mathis. He thought of trying to get a ride to the county seat, to call from there. But it was late, already ten o'clock. He decided he had better go to Mister Tittle.

"It good we got that burial," Cooter said.

"She sho have suffer her time," Louella said.

"I going get Mister Tittle telefome the burial," Albert said. "Lettie, you reckon you can go over yonder and get Preacher Tom?"

"I can go."

"Don't send Sistah," Louella said. "Cooter can go over there. I ruther Sistah stay here with me."

"Cooter fraid to go in the dark," Daniel said. "Ain't you, Cooter?"

"I ain't fraid to go. I ain't fraid, Papa."

They all went out of the house together. Lettie and Louella and Daniel followed Albert across the pasture and waited at the bottom of the lane. Once Albert looked back at the house. Sitting there at the edge of the pasture before the pine trees, the house looked small, like a toy house thrown aside by some careless hand. And the house looked as though no one had lived in it for a long, long time.

TEN

Ahead of Albert, Mister Tittle's house gleamed white as clean cotton. No light was burning and Albert went to the back, knocked on the door and called Mister Tittle's name.

"Hey?"

"This Albert, Mister Tittle. I see you a minute?"

"Hey?"

"I see you a minute, Mister Tittle? This Albert."

There was a silence. Then low voices whispered to each other. Soon Mister Tittle's feet struck the floor and he came to the door barefooted and shirtless. "Mother of us all, Prince. Is anybody sick?"

"The old woman, Mister Tittle. She dead."

"She died tonight?"

"Yessir. While we's gone."

Mister Tittle called this news in to Miss Mary and she mumbled some reply of surprise.

"You'll need to call that burial fellow," Mister Tittle said.

"Yessir." Albert pulled the burial policy from his pocket.

"You can get John Mathis to call. He'll charge the call to you."

Albert could not bring himself to tell Mister Tittle of what had happened at the store. He said, "I wonder would you call, Mister Tittle? And talk to the burial yo'self. Mama down there in the pastah just with Lettie."

"Has Mathis closed the store yet?"

"Yessir. Least-a-ways the lights off."

"I'll get my shoes on and go to Mathis' house. Is there anything else you'll need to do?"

"I don't s'pose. The burial folks take care of things."

"She got no relatives to notify?"

"They just Mama, far's we know."

A car came up the road. Its headlights were dim, like two shrunken yellow moons side by side.

"There Preacher Tom now," Albert said. "I go down to the house with him, then come back."

Milo Johnson, going home late, with no sign of his wife Belle with him, had caught a ride on the car, but when it turned he jumped off the fender and disappeared into the night.

Albert returned within an hour but had to wait thirty minutes before Mister Tittle came up.

"They can't locate the burial company. They say the telephone's been disconnected." Mister Tittle shook his head. "But John Mathis acted funny."

Albert did not say anything.

"Probably something out at that store," Mister Tittle said, talking to himself. He looked down at the burial policy he still held in his hand. "You go on back. People will be coming. I'll go up there and call again first thing in the morning."

Mister Tittle tried all Sunday morning to locate the burial company. In the afternoon he called a cousin who lived in Jackson. At sundown the cousin telephoned back to say that the company had moved. "But I can't find out where. And I've checked everywhere I know to check."

"It's a hell of a note," Mister Tittle told Albert as they stood at the edge of the yard beside the crape-myrtle bushes. "But if you'll come up here early in the morning I'll take you down to Gibbsburg and let you talk to the sheriff. He'll be able to help us out."

Albert remembered that Mister Mathis planned to go to the county seat on Monday, too. He moved about the edge of the crape-myrtle bushes, plucking leaves from the trees and crushing them in his hand, and looking at Mister Tittle out of the corners of his eyes.

"John Mathis will be glad if I let his phone alone, anyway. The way he acted all day. I don't know what's come over that man."

"You charge the fome, Mister Tittle?"

"I gave him cash."

"I sho give it back when we gin."

A wagon loaded with people came from the road and turned toward the lane. In the wagon were R-Rula and her husband Bull, who had come up from New Orleans where he worked; Cindy, thin as a dime, whom everybody said had t.b., with her daughter Daisy; Tilda with her crippled daughter and some man from Crossville; Aunt Rosa, who held a cake in a towel on her lap; Solo Thompson; and a dozen children. They were all on their way to the wake but stopped upon seeing Albert.

"E'nin, Prince."

"E'nin, you-all." Albert stopped pulling the leaves from the crape-myrtle bushes. "You-all can drive on down to the house. Mama and them all there."

The wagon moved on and was followed by R.A., who was helping Uncle Scott to walk. Uncle Scott stumbled along with his eyes watching his feet and he was forever mumbling something to R.A. But except to keep the old man from falling R.A. paid him no attention.

"Uncle Scott's got no business going down there," Mister Tittle said.

"It the truth. But you know he going, it the last thing he ever do."

Augustus came then, with Jenny. He walked over to Albert while Jenny waited near the head of the lane.

"I be on, Mama," Augustus said. "In a little while with Prince."

"You come on. You come on here with me."

Augustus went on with her.

Over at the sawmill some white men, Mister Dillard and three others, sat on a low pile of lumber talking loud and passing the early evening. Now and then they tilted their heads back and laughed hard.

On the road a truck roared past to leave a boiling funnel of dust hanging in the air.

And just now the bell in the steeple of the Baptist Church began to toll the hour for evening services. Mister Tittle looked at a great round watch he drew from a pocket. "Roberts is ringing a little early."

Albert began to move about again, but made himself stop.

"I'll feed and milk tonight," Mister Tittle said.

"Yessir." Albert hesitated but forced himself to say, "And I be up here by day in the mornin. To go down yonder."

They drove to Gibbsburg in Mister Tittle's car, an old-model Chevrolet which Miss Mary always made certain was polished and in proper repair. Mister Tittle did not drive fast and they were not on the road five minutes when Mister Mathis blew his car horn behind them and flew past in his Buick. Mister Tittle lifted his hand in greeting. But Mister Mathis clung to the steering wheel and stared straight ahead.

Mister Tittle chuckled quietly. "Guess John's eyes are going bad."

Beyond Crossville Mister Tittle stopped the car

and waited while Albert went across a field to tell Hollis Darty, Louella's stepfather, of the old woman's death, and it was near ten o'clock when they drove up to the courthouse in Gibbsburg.

The courthouse was a gray stone building with high dark windows. Beside the courthouse stood the jailhouse and Albert saw the spot where, fifteen years before, he and Louella had been married. But it was near an old cannon, grown rusty since World War I, beside a truck, that Mister Tittle parked the car. Beyond the truck, and Albert did not see it until he stepped out of the car, was Mister Mathis' Buick.

Albert hesitated.

"You come on in, Prince," Mister Tittle said.

They were going up the courthouse steps, past the men who sat chewing tobacco, when Mister Mathis came out the door.

Mister Tittle stopped. "Good morning, John."

Mister Mathis kept on walking.

"God Almighty," Mister Tittle swore.

The sheriff was Mister Ike Mason, a powerful man with a great bulging stomach that lay atop his belt and pushed his trousers down so far they appeared always about to fall from his hips. On his right hip hung a black-barreled, pearl-handled revolver in a black leather holster. The holster flapped low against Mister Mason's thigh when he walked in his hard, determined gait, as though rushing forward to some pressing piece of business. His face was ruddy and his eyes were round as two green muscadines, and so large they made him always appear surprised. He sat on the top of his desk with one leg drawn crooked and hidden beneath his stomach.

"Good morning, Ike."

"Come on in, John. Good to see you."

Some people said Mister Ike Mason was twenty times a politician for every time he was a sheriff.

Albert started to follow Mister Tittle through the door, but Mister Mason stopped him. "You wait outside, boy." And then to Mister Tittle: "How's the crop this year, John?"

"Fair. Fair crop, I guess. I just came down to bring Prince Albert there. He's having a little trouble."

"I already heard about it." Mister Mason raised his voice. "What happened, boy?"

Albert looked through the door at Mister Tittle, then back to the sheriff. "The old woman, Mama's gran'mama, died on a Sadday. We has the burial, but ain't been able to get them word."

"Is that all you came down here for?"

"Yessir."

"Is that all, John?"

"That's all. Prince wanted to see if you might be able to locate the burial company. It moved, and nobody can find out where."

Mister Mason stared at them with the look of surprise in his eyes. "Did you just see John Mathis leaving here?"

Albert wished that he had made himself speak to Mister Tittle before they arrived at the sheriff's office. He dug his hands into his pockets.

"I saw him at the door," Mister Tittle said. "He seemed in a pretty big hurry."

"He's been in a hurry. He's been with the chancery clerk since early. And a little while ago Rawlins and Mathis came down to talk to me. Rawlins is back upstairs now, finishing up the papers."

"Papers for what?" Mister Tittle said.

"For what? Lien papers against that boy's crop. Mathis is taking a lien on what that boy makes."

"A lien?" Mister Tittle looked at Albert. "Lord God, man. What for?"

"For the debt that nigger owes. You owe him, don't you, boy?"

"Yessir, I do."

"Well, I'll be damn," Mister Tittle said. "I'll just be damn." His eyes began to flash in their piercing way. "What'd John Mathis do that for?"

"He said they had a run-in at the store Saturday."

Through a door at his side Albert could see the jailhouse and the dark figure of some man who clung to the heavy bars across a small high window. He shook his head. "Ain't been no run-in, Mister Tittle. Mister Mathis just cut my credit off. Say he ain't going furnish me no mo."

The sheriff clapped his hands across his stomach with an air of thoughtful authority. "John Mathis said he had no idea in this world what this nigger'd try to do next."

"Well, I'll just be damn," Mister Tittle said, and with these words turned toward the door as though he had reached some sudden decision. But he stopped, and went back into the office.

"About this other business, Ike. Could you find out about that burial company? Where they moved?"

"Well, now, I don't know. . . ." A fly crawled across Mister Mason's cheek toward his mouth; he slapped at the fly with the palm of his hand. "I can call the law in Jackson. And see if they can find out where the company moved to."

"I'd appreciate your doing it," Mister Tittle said. He abruptly bade the sheriff good day and went down the hall.

"Come back in and see me, John," Mister Mason called.

Mister Tittle did not pause or look back. "Thank you, Ike."

While they rode back to Longfield Albert told Mister Tittle all that had happened at the store. Mister Tittle listened silently, but he drove the car faster than Albert had ever seen him drive; the car bounced on the rutted gravel road and the back wheels skidded around the sharp curves and slung rocks off into adjoining ditches. Before they arrived at Longfield they overtook Mister Mathis. Mister Tittle blew the car horn, not lifting his hand now and not smiling, and they sped on past. Mister Tittle did not speak again until he stopped the car. "I guess you'll have to wait, to see what Ike can do."

"Yessir."

Albert waited for Mister Tittle to say something more. But Mister Tittle slammed the car door and went inside the house.

Albert stood beside the barn, talking with Augustus and R.A. It was already one o'clock, and no word had come from Mister Mason or the burial company when Lettie came up the lane.

"Prince, Sistah say why ain't you come on to the house. Say Preacher Tom say he ready."

"Tell Mama we waitin. Tell her we be there when they come."

At two-thirty Jesse Darver sped up in the hearse, and was followed by a car and a pickup truck. Jesse's head was shining with sweat and his dark suit held a light layer of dust.

"I sorry we ain't been got yo word sooner," he said. "We done move us office Sadday and ain't had us new telefome hooked in. I sho sorry you-all been waitin."

Albert was too proud that the hearse had come at last to say anything.

"Where you-all bury?" Jesse said.

"Hill of Mount Zion. Preacher Tom going hold the funeral."

"The grave already dug," Augustus said. "Solo and them been up there diggin ever since early mornin."

They all went down to the tenant house. Everyone Albert knew was there. They sat packed on the porch and stood waiting in the yard. They stood in the shade of the peach tree and out beside the lot.

Near the chimney Old Reuben stood talking to Aunt Molly Paterson. Aunt Molly fanned herself with an old palmetto fan, nodded her head up and down and glanced archly about the yard. It was easy to see she did not listen to a word Old Reuben said.

Out at the water well Tilda drew a bucket of water and gave her daughter a drink from a tin dipper dented on the bottom. Big Sam, R-Rula's dog, came out from under the house and lapped at water that Tilda spilled. Some children who had been playing in the shade of the sweet-gum tree stopped their games and stared curiously at the hearse.

Albert went inside the house, where people stood in small groups talking quietly. Many of the women had brought flowers picked from their yards and tied with string—bright-orange marigolds with their ragged leaves, bunches of pale-blue and pink button zinnias, and larger zinnias in bouquets red, yellow, white and lavender. There were red and white roses, already shattering, and a large bouquet of purple dahlias sent by Coralee Timmons, Myrabell's aunt who was paralyzed in her legs. The flowers had been put into quart fruit jars holding water and placed against the wall. The smell of the flowers mingled with the odor of sweet pomade which glistened in the women's hair.

In the kitchen, spread out on the table, were chicken bones, the remaining pieces of some pies and the crumbling last slices of some cakes. Albert ate a piece of pie and a slice of cake while Louella stood at his elbow.

"I put that piece of meat back in the stove," she said, and added, "So's the ants won't get at it."

"Augustus helpin them?"

"He helpin. They puttin her in it now."

"I going need me some clean ov'alls."

"I already put yo other pair there on the chair."

Aunt Rosa stuck her head in at the door. "They going be ready now."

The coffin had been loaded into the hearse. Belle and Minnie Sue took the flowers out and everyone gathered around the front porch, on both sides of the steps. They did not talk, but waited solemnly, with the hot sun on their heads. Relative had gathered near to relative, and yet, here in the presence of death, they all somehow stood separately too, as though strangers to one another.

Aunt Molly lowered her old voice and whispered into Albert's ear. "You and yo folks ride in the burial car. Preacher Tom can follow after that."

Jesse Darver waited for a signal. Soon Preacher Tom lifted his hand.

The hearse pulled forward, was followed by the car Albert rode in, and Preacher Tom pulled into line. Behind Preacher Tom's car came a wagon loaded with people, and behind the wagon all the others walked, making a long procession that moved slowly across the pasture and up the lane.

When the procession passed near the corner of Mister Tittle's house Albert saw Miss Mary watching from behind the screened front door. But Mister Tittle was nowhere in sight.

Uncle Scott, whom no one had remembered to give a ride, had been walking, with difficulty, far in the rear. But now he stopped, with no one at his side, as though unable to go any farther. For a moment he stood in the middle of the road, a solitary figure, watching all the others move away from him. He lifted his arm after them and tried to follow. But Albert saw him stumble and fall on the hard gravel. And then there went Mister Tittle, out to the road to help the old man up.

"Sit still, Daniel," Albert said.

The hearse crept forward in low gear, so that those walking could follow, and the procession moved on, winding along the narrow road among the pine trees toward the cemetery.

ELEVEN

ALBERT LEFT the tenant house at daybreak next morning and went to Mister Tittle's barn without breakfast. He milked, saving back the quart of strippings for his calf, and was ready to leave the barn when Mister Tittle came up.

"I want to go to the store this morning, before you go to the field."

"Sir?"

"Don't go to the field yet. I want to go up to see John Mathis."

"I don't want you go to no troubles, Mister Tittle. I can just go on out the credit. I can just try and go on like that. Mister Mathis told me get out that sto."

"I told you to go on and paint the house because the house is mine and you wanted to paint it. I don't guess John Mathis would understand that. But there are some other things he may understand."

They found Mister Mathis on the store porch unlocking the gasoline pump.

"Good morning, John," Mister Tittle said.

"John," Mister Mathis replied.

Mister Tittle moved over to the edge of the store porch. "Hot as hell already."

Mister Mathis did not reply.

The black cat came through a hole in the screen door behind Mister Mathis and rubbed against Mister Mathis' leg.

"That cat any good for rats?" Mister Tittle asked.

"Tol'able."

Both men were silent for a time, as though each of them waited for the coming of a certain respectful moment when they could release the pent-up words that lay behind their faces. Albert shifted his feet.

"What's this about Prince Albert, John?" Mister Tittle said at last.

"I stopped his credit."

"Hasn't been buying too much, has he?"

"I cut his credit off."

"You know he's in the middle of his crop?"

Mister Mathis moved his hand so that the diamond ring sparkled in the sunshine. "Middle of the crop or no crop at all, I stopped it."

"You took a lien on the crop, too?"

"I sure did." Mister Mathis began to pump gasoline. "He owes me money."

Albert saw Mister Tittle's eyes begin to move in
their bright way. "Never failed to pay you before,
has he?"

"No telling what may happen, though."

"That's part my crop down there, John. He works
on halves."

Mister Mathis pushed the gasoline pump handle
in and out, in and out, using his arm fast as a piston.
"I got a right to a lien on anything he makes down
there. That's law. For the debt he owes. I mean what
he makes, not what belongs to you."

"You do it because he's planning to paint that
house?"

Mister Mathis pumped gasoline at a rapid pace.
The glass service tank was already full and now
gasoline began to gurgle into the overflow pipe and
run back into the big drums underground. The sunshine slanting into the filled tank lay caught by the
curved tank surface so that a bright spot the size
and color of an orange had formed, a miniature sun
which threw its own rippling bright light across the
dark cement flooring of the porch.

"You can say that," Mister Mathis said. "You can say that."

Both men were again silent for a time.

Above Mister Tittle's eyes small beads of moisture glistened in the sunshine. He took a handkerchief from his pocket and wiped at his forehead. Then he moved the handkerchief back and forth before his face, trying to stir up a little breeze. Finally he said, "You've certainly acted hastily. Taking a lien, and expecting money from a crop when you're trying to stop the means for the crop being made. My God, man, it's like you're standing yourself up with one hand and knocking yourself down with the other. You thought of that?"

The passenger train thundered past and a moment later Howard Dauber, Mister Dauber's son, came by dragging the dusty mailbag along the center of the road. The mailbag left in its wake a wide smooth path that divided the road into two halves.

"I've thought of more than that," Mister Mathis said. "Some things you'd better think about yourself. You know that nigger's not just painting a house. You know that well as me, and everybody else around here. You see how they all met down there last Saturday. Every nigger around here knows what he's doing. You've got to realize that painting that house means a lot more than you think it does."

"I've been knowing all along," Mister Tittle said.

"And you'll let him do it?"

"If he can get his paint and do his painting. Yes."

Mister Mathis' face grew red. "You'd better think about it some more."

"I've already thought."

"But maybe not enough," Mister Mathis said. "Painting that house would just be the beginning of what would happen next. How many times have we seen that? Plenty, I can tell you. If they manage to make a clear dollar, they spend two and charge three. And then they leave. I've lost a lot of money with them leaving, too. If you let this business get out of hand they'll all start thinking they're good as you or me. So I'm going to stop this thing. If somebody don't, a man can't say where it all would end."

"You're going beyond all reason, John," Mister Tittle said. "By your cussed blindness, you're doing it."

"Blind?" Mister Mathis' head doddered like a baby's. "If I couldn't see——"

"You're doing it," Mister Tittle said. "You know why that mill has run off and on, mostly off, for the last few years. It's because George Dauber can't find anybody to cut logs. No good timber around here like there used to be. But there are still logs to be cut. And look at the land lying idle around here, not being used for two or three years now. Look at Merrill Roberts' place, with about half of his land in cultivation because he can't get any hands. Look at the Dickens' place. This is hard land anyway, but without planting at all . . .

"And why is all that? Because people are drifting off, like you said. But hell-fire, man, I don't see any sense in trying to scare off the ones who're staying. Can't you in your blindness see that before long there won't be anybody left?"

"It's not *my* blindness worries me."

"It had better worry you, for your own good. Where's your business coming from when everybody leaves? The attitude you take and the things you do will ruin this town for good. Ruin it not just for some, and you don't know it. But ruin it for everybody, and you don't know that, either. It's like you're standing yourself up with one hand and knocking yourself down with the other."

"Every last one that has left here has left owing——"

"It's not who's left I'm talking about. You're making things hard for everybody. Yourself, too, and you let your hate blind you. Stopping Prince Albert's credit makes it bad here in the middle of a crop."

"But I stopped it."

Mister Tittle's eyebrows gathered like two black caterpillars hunched facing each other. Beneath the caterpillars his eyes glinted like the sharpened steel point of a plow. He stood as though his feet had taken root in the hard red gravel.

"Don't I stand for what he gets?"

"Not now, you don't. You sure as hell don't."

Mister Tittle cursed under his breath.

Mister Mathis strained to hear, listening like a spring robin, his head thrust forward and to one side, as though, without using his hand, he cupped his ear.

"Well, damn it all," Mister Tittle said, "I trade up here."

"And your credit's good. But not his. And not his with you standing for it. We'll see how long it takes him to get some sense in his head."

The two men stared at each other.

"That's my goddamn house, John!"

"And it's my goddamn groceries!"

Mister Tittle controlled his temper by turning

sharply on his heels and walking off down the road. Albert followed him, but the other did not speak until they stood beside the barn.

"John Mathis is a funny man, Prince." Mister Tittle's voice had calmed and was thoughtful. "When he first came here that church up there had been dead for two years. People went to church at Crossville then. But with his own money he hired Brother Sutton to preach. Got the church going again and it's been going ever since. And Mathis seldom misses a sermon.

"But he's a stubborn man, a man who hates any kind of change whatever. He still sees this town the way he saw it the first year he owned that store. Eighteen long years, and he's thinking the same he did then, refusing to let himself know what's changing before his very eyes. But because he owns that store people have sort of let him run and rule. Him and a few others. And they've made a mess of it. A mess a man hates to have his hand in."

"Yessir," Albert said gravely. "I ain't meant——"

"But a man's got to stand against that kind of blindness, if he wants to live on on his land."

"Yessir."

Mister Tittle spoke quietly. "This land is mine

and that house is mine. And if you still want to, you go ahead with what you're trying to do."

"I yet got that calf to sell."

"How much does he weigh now?"

"He going to'ad two hundred, I reckon. He going be ready to sell time I lay by."

"What the hell are you selling him then for?"

"He eatin so much, Mister Tittle."

"For three months you've fed him every drop of Miss Mary's cream. There's no use to stop now. And you might as well go ahead and feed him that ten acres of corn we have over there. He'd probably weigh four hundred pounds by the time you gin."

Albert grinned. "He would, Mister Tittle. Yessir, he sho would."

"Well, you could see," Mister Tittle said in parting.

Albert got the bridle to catch Mac. While he harnessed the mule he thought deep in his mind about the things Mister Tittle and Mister Mathis had said. He hated that what he wanted to do had caused them to argue. But he knew that Mister Tittle was right.

"They some folks leavin, Mac. They is. But then they some folks ain't."

Mac blinked his round eyes as though understanding why some people might leave and some might stay.

Albert adjusted the backband and nodded. Mister Tittle was right about the calf, too. The calf would weigh four hundred pounds by fall, if Old Bertha did not decide to have a calf of her own too soon. Albert gave the mule's broad neck a brisk slap.

"Step right, now. Me and you late already."

TWELVE

OFTEN, during the week after the argument at Mister Mathis' store, Albert went to the opening beside the creek to drink water from the brown jug he kept shaded with sweet-gum leaves at the base of the pine tree. His mouth would be dry. The suspenders of his overalls would be sticking to his back like two crossed strips of tape. He would wipe the sweat from his face and drink the shade-cool water, stale with the taste of the corncob stopper.

But there beside the tree that sent its searching roots far down into the land he did not mind the taste of the water. And in his field he did not mind the way he gave his strength to his work with more vigor than he had ever known. He urged the mule up and down the rows feeling as though he walked some narrow line. The field was neat and weedless.

One day at noontime he went home for his dinner.

The day was still; there was no wind. He found
Louella in the bedroom putting on her shoes. "Where
you going, Mama?"

She looked at him and he saw the sadness in her
eyes.

"Where you going?"

"You know them white mens met last night?"

"What they meet for?"

"Preacher Tom say he don't know. Say he just
know they met, up there to Mister Mathis' sto.
Preacher Tom say ain't been Mister Mathis ask them
neither. Say it been Mister Tittle."

"Mister Tittle ain't said nothin."

"Ain't going say nothin, neither. That meetin
white folks' business."

She straightened her dress and went into the
kitchen.

Albert followed her. "Where you going?"

"I going up the road. Soon's I dip these collards
for yo dinner. Ain't nothin for yo dinner cep these
collards. Them chillun eat the last of the bread."

"I ain't so hungry."

"I don't know what we going do, lessen you go on
up there to Mister Tittle."

"Mister Tittle know how things is. He do somethin when the time come."

"The time come? The time done here. He say go on with the house, can you do it by yo'self, but that cotton his and yo's both. He pendin on you in that crop. And he s'pose to see you get yo furnish."

"Mister Tittle know what he doing. He know them folks better'n us. But you ain't said where you going."

"Going up yonder to see Miss Maureen, you just got to know. Going see do her washin need doing."

"I don't want you go up there."

"I reckon I can go."

Something moved inside Albert. He went across the kitchen and stood behind her with his arms around her waist.

"You better eat these collards."

"Don't go up yonder, Mama."

"I going, now. You can just stop yo talkin."

The quietness of the day entered the kitchen. The mockingbirds did not sing in the sweet-gum tree; Old Bertha's bell did not sound from the pasture. Nothing moved. The day held itself paused, as though listening. Albert wished for words to tell

Louella how his heart twisted, but he possessed only a silence, a silence that spread out over the land until it joined the stilled hushed day itself. He tightened his arms about her.

"I get you in some wood and water," he said.

Late that afternoon the smothering stillness passed. Dark clouds formed in the east. They mounted the sky and threw their thunder over the land. A wind came up. The wind bowed the tops of the cornstalks, rustling the wide bright leaves into a whisper that moved across the field like the distant hum of bees. Soon the sun was hidden and birds sought out their early roost. The earth lay dark green beneath a threatening sky.

When Albert came from the field to the house he saw Daniel squatting beside the chimney digging a hole with a rusted tablespoon. "Daniel! Don't dig up the yard. You already put too many holes in this yard."

"Ain't me doing it, Papa."

"Who is it, then?"

"It a gopher, Papa. It a big black gopher comin in here diggin these holes. Last night me and Cooter heard him. Heard him grittin his teeth and diggin."

"I know the gopher doing the diggin. You come on here with me."

Albert took Daniel's hand and they went to the front porch where Preacher Tom and Augustus sat with Lettie and Louella. Albert searched Louella's face for some sign of what Miss Maureen had said. But Louella was talking and did not stop.

"They sho met," she said.

"They did," Preacher Tom said.

"What you-all hear?" Lettie said.

They went on talking, though Albert could tell that they directed their words to him; it was for him that they related again what they had heard and already discussed.

"R-Rula been still dryin the dishes when Mister Dauber come in. She heard Mister Dauber talkin bout the mens meetin. Say the mens was first cam, then mad. Say they been cussin cause of the way Mister Tittle actin. Him and Mister Roberts. R-Rula say it just like them mens ain't doing nothin but knockin they heads."

"You hear that, now!" Lettie said.

"Pearl say Mister Mathis come way from that sto with his head lookin like a apple," Preacher Tom said. "Red like that. Say he mumbled to hisself, then

163

riz his voice sayin the name of Mister Tittle. Pearl say she ain't never seen no man actin so vi'lent and yet ain't fightin nobody. Mister Mathis had to go right on to bed. And Miss Mathis sunt Pearl on, fo she heard no mo."

Little by little, as they talked on, Albert began to form a picture of what must have happened at the meeting. The men had talked about the same things Mister Mathis and Mister Tittle had argued about that day on the porch of the store. Tempers had come up like quick little mice from a hole, then had scooted out of sight again. But the men had not agreed; they had not settled anything among themselves.

Albert did not know what to think of it all. He sat troubled while the clouds, growing darker, built up until they touched the roof of the sky and came sloping across the land as though tumbling down a hill. The wind whipped the branches of the peach tree against one another, swept dust over the yard and sent the water-well bucket clattering along the ground until it hung at the end of the rope. Lightning like big red pencil marks streaked the sky.

Augustus stepped down into the yard. "Let's go for a walk, Lettie."

"You see how it blowin up a storm, Augustus."

"We ain't going go far. I wantin talk with you."

"She don't want to take no walk, Augustus," Preacher Tom said. As he spoke a gust of wind lifted his hat from his head. The hat rolled through the front door and went out of sight inside the house.

Augustus scowled. "I ain't ask you go no walkin."

"I just sayin," Preacher Tom said.

"You right. You just sayin."

"Amen."

"You don't have do no sayin, when they ain't nobody dressin you. You best save yo voice for them sermons."

Lettie giggled. "You hush that talk, Augustus."

"Let him talk," Preacher Tom said. "They just ain't nobody wantin take no walk."

Augustus clenched his fists and took two steps toward the preacher. "I can do mo'n talk."

Preacher Tom stood bravely.

"Don't you-all carry on that-a-way," Albert said. "You go in the house, Lettie."

Augustus took another step forward.

"Remember the Lawd," Preacher Tom said.

Albert placed himself between the preacher and Augustus, and said, "I don't want you-all startin no troubles at my house, Augustus. You and Preacher Tom. This my house where Mama and the boys live. I done spoke with Lettie. Cidin what to do have to be her business, but don't neither you-all start no troubles here at my house."

"You right, Prince," Augustus said. "You right." He turned and went off across the pasture.

"The Lawd know he right," Preacher Tom said. He swayed on the heels of his feet and for a moment it appeared that he might suddenly rise on a big gust of wind and go sailing out across the tops of the trees like some strange wild bird.

Daniel ran onto the porch. "Here yo hat, Preacher Tom. It roll in yonder under the bed."

"I thank you, Daniel." Preacher Tom glanced at Albert. "The Lawd bless you and yo house, Prince. I be going on, now."

"Good e'nin, Preacher Tom."

Inside the house the wind whistled through the cracks of the walls and flapped the cardboard papering; the wind banged the shutters closed, then opened them again; it gushed down the chimney and flurried the old ashes on the hearth. A white sheet of something sailed through the front door. When lightning

flashed Albert recognized the whiteness in mid-air—
a piece of old newspaper that whipped into the bedroom and hung against the wall.

"You better close them shutters," Louella said,
"fo this house blow off." She ran from room to room,
calling for Cooter, who did not answer. "Daniel! Go
yonder and close that shutter!"

Louella latched the shutter herself and hurried
from room to room again, hunting Cooter. "Cooter!"
she yelled. "Cooter!" But she could not find Cooter
and went back to the kitchen muttering for Daniel to
stand out of the way.

Lettie sat slumped into a chair drawn near the
hearth. She did not notice Albert, or, seeing him,
did not look up. He stood above her, behind her
chair, thinking a moment before he spoke. "You see
what like to happen out there?"

"I seen it."

"They done start hatin each other, cause of you.
And you going have do somethin. Make up yo mind
bout them. I ain't wantin folks be fightin at my house.
This house need be right on the inside. It got to be
good on the inside, well as the outside. You understand what I sayin?"

"I ain't want them start fightin."

"You leave Sistah lone," Louella called from the kitchen. "Sistah ain't done nothin."

Albert went into the kitchen. "Lettie need a talkin to, Mama. Making them act the way they do's."

"They ain't going fight. Augustus just showin off. Tryin scare Preacher Tom."

"It ain't right, though." Albert sat beside the stove and the wind drew the warm odor of the boiling collards past his face. He could see that Louella was nervous and he waited several minutes before he asked her if she had seen Miss Maureen.

"I seen her."

"Her washin need doing?"

"She say it don't."

"She may got somebody else."

"I don't know. She stood at that screen out lettin me in the house. Say well, well, well. Then she just laugh."

A strong gust of wind howled around the corner of the house. A streak of lightning flashed near by and the rumble of thunder that followed sounded like speeding trucks passing over a wooden bridge. Daniel hugged against Louella.

"Miss Maureen ought not to did that," Albert said.

"She did it, though. Didn't even let me come inside and rest a little. Get back, Daniel!"

"I scared, Mama."

"I told Miss Maureen I sho needin the work mighty bad, could she use me. She just laugh some mo, shakin. Then she say she ain't wantin her washin done by me for nothin. Say she do the washin herself fo she let me do it. So I just come on. It make me mad them folks laugh in my face like she done."

"I ain't want you go up there noways."

"Go on, Daniel!" Louella pushed Daniel aside. "Miss Maureen know I put out a good washin. It likely she just done run out them dresses she been payin me with. Actin like she done. I just don't trust them folks!"

A streak of lightning cracked over the house like a whip. A crash, as of timber falling, came from the front.

"That hit somethin," Albert said, and ran out to the porch. The shed over the water well had been struck down. The two-by-fours and the platform which held the water bucket lay across the ground.

Back in the house Daniel screamed. Albert hurried back to the kitchen. His son crouched against the wall holding the side of his head. Albert was beside him with a single step. "What the matter with you?"

"I told him get out the way," Louella said. She stood with her hands on her hips, her feet a little apart.

"Mama slap me, Papa. Side the head."

Albert lifted Daniel into his arms. "You ought not to hit him, Mama."

Louella's face loosened and sagged, looking old in the lamplight. "They don't nothin go right. They ain't nothin in this house but collards and you keep on waitin for Mister Tittle. Them mens meetin, don't nobody know what for, and Miss Maureen doing that way. Then Daniel just stay in the way all time. It just get my nerves on a razzle. Like it makin a wreck of me."

Albert sat on the bench holding Daniel on his knee. Now, for the first time, he noticed that the storm was passing. The wind had died down and the lightning came from far away.

"You ain't hurt him much, Mama," he said. "Is she, Daniel?"

"Nosir."

When Louella put the collards on the table Albert believed he saw a dampness in her eyes. So that she would not know he noticed this, he turned to Lettie. "Where Cooter?"

"He out yonder with that calf."

"He been out there all this time?"

"I reckon he is. Say he don't want nothin happen to that calf."

Cooter came up the back steps and into the kitchen. He was grinning. "He all right, Papa. They ain't nothin hurt him."

"You come on here to yo supper, Cooter," Louella said. "You got no business out there in that rickety shed when the wind been blowin so."

Albert drew out the bench for Louella to sit. And while they ate, Albert still heard the distant rumble of thunder.

THIRTEEN

THE NEXT MORNING Cooter began to carry armloads of wood into the kitchen. Albert noticed that now, for the first time in his life, his son went about this task without needing to be reminded of it. Cooter stacked his arms with loads that would have been a strain for Albert himself and went staggering off to the kitchen where, with a certain grave eagerness, he piled the wood in a box beside the stove. Sticks of wood spilled from the box onto the floor. Albert turned his head away.

Louella moved out of Cooter's path. "Have mercy, Cooter. What done come over you?"

Albert went out to the lot to see his calf. While he rubbed his hand over the sleek red hair, feeling the smooth ripple of muscles beneath, a thought came to him: he must sell the calf. A moment later he dismissed this idea with a shrug. That night, after long thought, he knew that he must go to Mister Tittle.

But early Friday morning Miss Mary came down to the tenant house. She held a tray covered with a white napkin in the crook of her arm and carried a molasses bucket in her hand. Miss Mary looked out of place coming across the yard; it was the first time she had been to the tenant house since she came to doctor Louella, sick with a cold, eight years before.

"Mornin, Miss Mary," Albert said.

"Good morning, Albert." Her eyes moved over the house. "Here are some things I brought. Some milk, and things."

He took the tray into his hands carefully, fearing he would drop it. "We sho thank you, Miss Mary."

"Mister Tittle's going down to Gibbsburg as soon as he gets the flat fixed. He wants you to make out a list of the groceries you need."

"Yes'm, Miss Mary. Yes'm. We get it ready." He called in to Louella. "Mama? Mama! Bring out a pencil. Miss Mary say Mister Tittle makin rangement to get us grocery."

"He wants you to put down enough for two weeks," Miss Mary said. "He can't afford to make trips down there every week."

Daniel kept his eyes fastened on the tray. "What you brung under that rag, Miss Mary?"

"You ask Louella, Daniel. And don't you mess with it."

"No'm."

Louella came out with a pencil and a piece of brown cardboard that she, in her haste, had snatched from the wall.

"You can bring the tray and napkin back any time." Miss Mary paused and looked at the house again. "When you get the list ready, bring it up to Mister Tittle. He's fixing a flat. We don't know where he picked up the nail." She went back across the pasture.

"You make the list," Albert said to Louella, and watched her write on the cardboard: fifteen pounds of salt meat, a gallon of Louisiana molasses, a sack of flour, a five-pound sack of salt, a can of coffee, a ten-pound sack of sugar, two nickel boxes of matches and a gallon of coal-oil, four bars of laundry soap, and a box of baking powder and a box of soda.

Albert went up the lane and presented the list to Mister Tittle. "You read the writin, Mister Tittle?"

The other nodded. "I've waited about doing this, Prince, until we had a meeting up there. But we didn't get anything settled. So I'll get your furnish-

ings down at Gibbsburg. Come back about dinner-
time and I'll have the things you need."

"Yessir, Mister Tittle. Yes*sir*."

When Albert returned to the tenant house Solo
Thompson sat on the porch with a hamper of beans
at his side. Solo wore a straw hat with the brim up
in the front and down behind. "I ain't got no time,
Prince. I just come by bringin you some beans."

"You make many this year, Solo?"

"This the first year I had beans, Prince. Folks
can't make no money with cotton and I cided try
some beans. But beans ain't worth nothin neither. I
took some down to Gibbsburg and they ain't give me
but a dollar a hamper. A man just can't raise no beans
for that. The fertilizer cost mo'n that make. The
next trip I went down there they ain't even want
the beans a-tall. Can't even give them folks the beans.
So I brung them back. A man just can't haul beans
for nothin. I been tryin sell a few round here. You
know, going from do' to do'. But don't nobody want
no beans.

"I just been tryin sell Jenny a hamper, over on the
road. Jenny say is I got any osh potatoes. Say she love
to have some osh potatoes. Osh potatoes, now! You
hear that? I told Jenny, 'Osh potato? What is a osh

potato? I don't even know no osh potato!' Comin at me askin for osh potatoes!"

Solo shook his head as though confounded, sighed loudly, then got up abruptly and went across the pasture with the brim of his hat beating against his neck. Albert could hear him mumbling, "Some folks! What is a osh potato? Just tell me that, Jenny. Just tell me that, if'n you can!"

Albert lifted the hamper and went inside, where Louella had taken the food from Miss Mary's tray and placed it on the table.

"I know Mister Tittle been knowin how things is."

"Seein you get yo grocery ain't no mo'n he s'pose to do," Louella said. "He s'pose to see you get the furnish when you workin on halves. But you better watch the figures on the things he get."

"Mister Tittle watch that."

They all sat to eat the fried chicken and biscuits and lemon pie and pickled peaches.

"Save back a little milk," Louella said. "So's we can have some in us coffee when Mister Tittle get back."

When they had finished, Albert rose from the table and said, "Come go with me, Mama."

"Where you going? To sit with that calf?"

"I going look at the cotton."

They walked down the steps and across the pasture, leaving Daniel and Cooter to pick at the chicken bones. Beneath the pine tree in the little clearing they stopped, and Albert said, "You stand here and wait for me. I be back."

He crossed the creek. As though sharing his feeling of joy, the cotton before him had begun to blossom wildly. Over all the field, from behind the wide dark leaves, scraps of white and pink and red shone out. He walked up and down the rows, measuring the growth of the cotton against his legs and stopping to pull back the thick leaves to count the squares on a stalk.

FOURTEEN

In July, after Albert laid the cotton by, there came the beginning of a middle time in the Piney Woods. He dug out the cotton sacks, gave their worn bottoms new patches and put the sacks in a handy place beneath the bed. He mended a part of the pasture fence that had been weakened by the wind in June, rebuilt the platform above the water well and helped Mister Tittle put some new shingles on the shed where Old Bertha would spend much of the winter.

These odd jobs seen after, he was free to seek public work, and one morning early he stood in the shade of the sweet-gum tree and spoke to Preacher Tom of going to Mister Dauber or Mister Dillard.

"I don't know," Preacher Tom said. "They do's funny. They no way of tellin if they put you on or not." His voice was lower than ever; it grew weaker and weaker, month in and out. Among several mem-

bers of Hill of Mount Zion there had come up the
question of calling another preacher. "Just no way
of tellin," he said, and with the toe of his shoe
thoughtfully urged an old gum ball around in a
circle.

"I better talk with Mister Tittle," Albert said.

Preacher Tom gave Albert a ride up the lane. The
preacher barely had the car under way before he
cleared his throat. "I don't like to say nothin, Prince.
But I been fraid they going be troubles, like I told
you there in the spring, if'n you member. I still fraid,
too. They some good mens round here, but you got
to think of Louella and yo chillun. And then that
trouble at yo house with Augustus. I hate things happen like that. Lettie young. She don't know how she
foolin Augustus on. Makin him act like he do."

"Lettie going stop her carryin on, Preacher Tom.
I done spoke with her."

"I glad to know you is. I like to see her leave
Augustus go on bout his business."

Preacher Tom gave his close attention to turning
the car from the pasture onto the lane. After all the
years of owning the car he continued to drive it
warily, as though he feared losing control of it. He
rounded the sharp corner without mishap and settled

back with a smile. When he let Albert out to see Mister Tittle he said, "I hope they put you on, Prince."

But Mister Tittle shook his head without any hesitation. "I doubt if they will."

"Back there in the spring Mister Dauber told me he sho want me to cut logs. Say they logs to cut."

"That was in the spring, though."

"Yessir."

"I wouldn't go up there."

"Nosir?"

"No. George Dauber wouldn't hire you. Or Dillard either. And there's no need to aggravate them."

"That debt in Gibbsburg going out of sight, I don't get some work."

"I still wouldn't go up there, though."

Mister Tittle pushed his hat back on his head and studied a penny he held in his fingers with long curiosity, a little glumly, not speaking.

Albert understood the other's silence and looked toward the sawmill, where a spray of orange sawdust curved into the sunshine like thin broom sedge swept by the wind. Beyond the saw, beneath some stacked lumber, R.A. sat with his hat off, catching a minute of rest out of sight of Mister Dillard, who just now crossed the mill yard with a cant hook on his shoul-

der. A sinking feeling came into Albert's stomach
as he watched Augustus hook a log and roll it forward. It was the last log in sight and minutes later the
mill stopped. R.A. came out from the stacked lumber; the men talked to one another for a time, then
began to leave the mill.

Albert turned to see that Mister Tittle had been
studying his face.

"We'll have cotton to pick soon, Prince."

"Yessir."

Albert did not return to the tenant house but sat
out beside the pasture with his back resting against a
fence post. Though he had never had a headache, one
came into his head now and throbbed above his eyes.
He picked up a dry twig, broke it into small pieces
and tossed the pieces at the toe of his outstretched
foot.

Soon Louella came out from the house wiping her
hands on her dress.

"Sit down with me, Mama."

She sat, not saying anything, but waiting, he knew,
for him to tell her what Mister Tittle had said.

"He say they won't hire me, I go up there."

"That ain't the wust of it, neither. They going
stop you paintin that house."

"I ain't going stop, though. Not long as Mister Tittle let me go on. And Mister Tittle ain't no man to change his mind back and forth."

Louella gazed across the pasture. "I just fraid, though. Them mens waitin. And it make me fraid, way they waitin they time."

"It make Papa mighty proud, he could know we went on with things."

"I fraid, though."

That afternoon Albert spent a long time standing beside the pine tree in the little opening near the creek. The sun shone hard against the tree and high in the air, against the blue of the sky, the pine needles glistened like threads of tinsel drawn together in an airy, shimmering bell.

Albert felt lost without work to do. He needed to be using his hands. The following morning, while the roosters crowed their waking, he took the crosscut saw across his shoulder and went to the woods. At the end of two weeks he had hauled enough wood to the tenant house, and to Mister Tittle, to last them both a full year.

August came then, bringing the humid heat of dog days. The days drew themselves out endlessly, all alike, and time passed through Albert's hands like water flowing over a single spot in the bed of a summer river. But sometimes the days were different.

Late one morning Lettie came running across the pasture with her dress belt flying behind her. Her face was covered with dust and her knees looked as though she had been crawling in gravel. She sat in a chair and began to cry.

"What the matter with you?" Louella said.

"They like to run over me."

"Who done that? Who?"

"Miss Mathis and Miss Dillard . . . in Miss Mathis' big car. I been walkin side the road, far's I could get out being in the ditch. Miss Mathis come drivin and I seen Miss Dillard pint her finger at me. Then them womens start laughin. And just when they got side of me they sot down on they horn. I jump and fell in the ditch. And they dust come all over me."

"You listen to that!" Louella said. She looked at Albert as though to prove some point.

"They say anythin?" Albert said.

"They ain't. Just run at me, blowin they horn."

"They going do mo'n somethin like that," Louella said angrily, directing her words to Albert. "I been tryin tell you."

Lettie shifted her shoulders. "They sho is. And you-all just sittin. They no tellin what they going do next. They sho ain't. It dange'ous us go yond that pastah. I don't feel like I going stand they carryin on, actin the way they do's. Scarin folks. It make me fraid stay round here."

Louella led Lettie into the bedroom.

"Why some folks don't want us paint the house, Papa?" Cooter said.

"I don't know. Some folks just funny."

Cooter's face grew serious as an old man's. He looked at his father gravely. "We do it though, Papa."

One day in September, while Albert shucked and shelled corn in Mister Tittle's barn, Augustus came up. "You hear bout the mill, Prince?"

"It down again?"

"Mo'n just that. That man from Bogolusa that own it come up here yestiddy and told Mister Dillard close that mill down for good. Say it ain't runnin steady enough to make no money. Say he reckon he just have to move it off to where he can get some logs."

Augustus climbed into the crib and helped Albert

shell the corn. "It make me just want to move off somewhere."

"You thought of farmin any, Augustus?"

"I have thought of it, Prince. But that farmin ain't so good. They don't nobody ever make nothin out of it round here. I been thinkin bout going up to Jackson. What you think of that?"

Albert watched the kernels of corn fall into a bucket at his feet. "That war took you off to some far places. You come back here, you get restless. And now the mill movin off. I don't reckon it hurt none to look bout, see what you find. You may can find you some place you like better'n here."

"They say a vet'an can get him a good job in Jackson, on the gov'ment trainin."

"You want to go, I reckon you ought to, Augustus. Don't, you ain't going have no satisfaction."

Augustus nodded. "How bout you, Prince? Folks makin things mighty hard for you. You ever think of leavin?"

"No, Augustus. This home to me. And they some folks ain't makin things hard. They some folks want me do what I aimin. I ruther stay on with them."

"You reckon Lettie would go with me?"

"I don't know bout that. Lettie been mad, though. And say she gettin fraid. She may be in mind to leave here. You have to see her bout it."

"I going make her go, I get her way from that preacher."

The mill moved away the following week and there remained only the sawdust pile, which sat in the September sun red as a clay hill. People passed it and frowned, but did not stop. Once children had mounted to its peak as though climbing to the top of the world; they had cried out at the view it gave of the town. They had tumbled down its steep sides with shouts and laughter, throwing its dust into little clouds. But now the children turned to other play; the sawdust pile sat forgotten.

One Sunday after the mill had been moved Augustus came to see Lettie. He had had his hair cut by Old Reuben and he wore a suit and a white shirt and a tie. He spoke to Albert and Louella and sat on the porch with them. They talked several minutes before Lettie came out and sat beside Augustus.

"Where you call yo'self been?" she asked Augustus.

"Not where I been, Lettie. It where I going."

"Where you going?" Louella said.

"To Jackson. Where they some work to do. But the truth, I hate to go up there by myself."

"Who you reckon going with you?" Lettie said.

Augustus grinned. "I don't know who likely go. I thought they may be somebody. You know, somebody go there and do my cookin."

Lettie walked out to the peach tree. She gave Augustus a sidelong glance and twirled around on her toes. "Why you lookin at me, Augustus?"

"I thought maybe you want to go off, too."

"Augustus!"

Albert remembered Louella as he had seen her that first day, when she had danced beneath the sweetgum tree in a yellow dress. He could see her clearly, her white teeth shining as she paused beside him, catching her quick breath, smiling, saying, "What yo name? . . ."

"You go, won't you?" Augustus said.

"Aw, Augustus."

Albert looked at Louella. He remembered the sunshine in their faces beside the jailhouse at the county seat, and thought of all their years together. He picked the years from his memory one by one, as he might sort seed corn, lingering over the good ones, tossing the bad ones back into a corner. He knew that

here in the Piney Woods were men who respected
him, and if he did not yet know his rightful place
among them, he believed he at least lived where that
place would at last be earned. He took the years up,
seeing them all, hearing Augustus' voice come from
far away.

"Will you go, now?"

"What you buy me, Augustus?"

"Buy you a silk dress, girl, and some high-heel
shoes."

The voices grew hushed again as Albert's thoughts
came down to the present. He held the present year
before him like a ball, turning it about in question.
He had seen Louella grow restless, and sometimes
afraid, and this worried him. But he had known from
the beginning that the year would not be an easy one
and he told himself he must be patient. He was
patient now, for it disturbed him to see Lettie acting as she did, unable to make up her mind about
Augustus.

"Yonder come Preacher Tom," Louella said.

"Sho is."

The preacher stopped the car beside the peach
tree and stood beside the opened door watching Lettie
as she moved to the porch to sit beside Augustus.

"I going, Augustus."

"Where you-all going?" Preacher Tom said.

"Up to Jackson, Preacher Tom," Augustus said.

"Lettie," Preacher Tom began, "I don't——"

"You can just hush," Lettie said. "I going." She spoke harshly, but as though to a father.

A sadness, as of long pain, came over Preacher Tom's face. He got back into his car and after some difficulty started the motor and drove away without looking again at Lettie.

"The ways of the Lawd," Cooter said.

"Papa is the Lawd," Daniel said, riding up on the handle of a broom.

"Daniel!"

Daniel laughed. "Well, he is, Cooter." He said, "Get up, mule," and went galloping around the corner of the house singing, "Papa is the Jesus Lawd! Papa is the Jesus Lawd!"

Augustus and Lettie left the porch and walked across the pasture toward the road. Louella thoughtfully watched them go.

"They could be us going off," she said. "Sistah just made up her mind cause she fraid to stay here in this house. Fraid of what them folks may going do."

"Let's go inside," Albert said.

They sat before the hearth. In the trees behind the house the katydids were singing. They had been singing for over a month, but now they sent out their noise by the hundreds. The sound made odd rhythms that lapped over one another, changed, and went on without ceasing.

"Hear them?" Albert said. "That cotton going soon be open."

FIFTEEN

THE CAR on the road passed slowly, almost stopped, and from his position beside the water well, without lifting or turning his head, Albert watched. He could see in the car Mister Jay, driving, and Mister Mathis. They had driven past twice already and Albert saw that they looked steadily toward the tenant house, as though searching for something.

He filled the jug he had brought from the field with water, pouring carefully, taking his time while the car turned and started past again. So that the men would not suspect he waited to see what they would do, he took the jug into the crook of his arm and went across the yard. But once out of sight he paused to listen. The only sound he heard was Louella's steps, bare feet on the loose boards, coming out to the porch. He went quickly to the corner of the house.

191

"You get the patch on that cotton sack, Mama?" he said, drawing her attention away from the road.

"Get it on? You took that sack with you to the field. This mornin. You ain't losin yo mind, is you? You know I give you the sack."

The car went on. Louella had not noticed it.

"You right, Mama. You is. It just slip my mind right then."

He decided, going back to the field, that Mister Mathis was concerned about the debt. Mister Mathis had probably wanted to ask about the crop, but had changed his mind for some reason. Albert would have been glad to tell him that he had picked and already ginned three bales of cotton. These were tagged and stacked on a platform beside the Gibbsburg gin and would be sold when the remaining bales were ready: Mister Tittle always liked to sell the entire crop at one time.

That time would not be far off. For after the slow days of mid-September a new activity had come to the Piney Woods. Men had called their families together and led them into the fields, where the opened cotton covered the land like a soft summer cloud. Light breezes had come already, and these rustled the leaves of the corn against each other dryly and pushed the scarecrow's hat down over his eyes.

A breeze blew now, against Albert's face as he stopped at the end of the cotton row and looked toward the cotton house where Daniel was visible through the door.

"Bring yo sack on, Daniel."

"What you say, Papa?"

"Come on here and help me and Cooter."

Daniel came down a row with a flour sack half full of cotton, some double handfuls he had taken from the pile Albert had already weighed and emptied.

Cooter began to pick faster. "I can low get this cotton, Daniel. You look at my sack there. You see. Me and Papa going. We just low-going."

"You ain't even got much as me," Daniel said.

Albert brushed some pieces of crushed cotton leaves from Daniel's head. "How come it, Daniel, you always be's so dirty in yo head?"

"I don't know, sir, Papa."

"You help Cooter bring his row on." And then: "Where you get that cotton in yo sack?"

"Pickin hind of Cooter, Papa. Cooter don't pick

193

no clean row." Daniel held his cotton sack above his head. "Looka here, Cooter. Look!"

Cooter would not look. This made Daniel mad and he began to throw himself round and round until he grew dizzy and fell.

"You stop that," Albert said. "You pickin cotton bout like that gopher comin in that yard diggin. You get yo'self on that row. How you think we going get over this field again, you sittin in that cotton house fillin yo sack? I ain't going tell you no mo start pickin."

"Yessir."

"I can pick a hundred pound a day," Cooter bragged.

"You can't, Cooter. But I can, though."

"The way you do? Playin like a baby."

Daniel's eyes grew round. "Papa can pick a hundred. He can pick three hundred."

"Listen to him, Papa. Listen to Daniel bleedin."

Daniel made a face at Cooter, then dived beneath some cotton leaves and went out of sight altogether.

While Albert picked along the row with the sun hard on his back his mind filled with thoughts of his house. He drew in a deep breath, thinking, and glanced behind him at Cooter and Daniel. They worked with their heads down, so he dropped his sack and slipped off into the woods.

He walked where the shade was heavy, where spots of sunlight trembled and moved when the wind stirred the branches overhead. Before him a yellow oriole soared up to the tip of a high beech limb where an old round nest hung swaying like a pine cone. The bird began to sing. And off to Albert's right, in a thicket of vines, a rabbit hopped up and hopped off, unseen.

He crossed the creek and at the edge of the pasture, shielded by the blue shade of a water oak, he sat with his legs crossed before him and looked at the house.

He had not been sitting long when he saw Louella run out onto the porch and bend her head toward the road. Beyond the house, and he could not see it from where he sat, a car started up and drove away. Its sound had faded when Louella flew into movement. She jumped off the porch as though frightened, holding the skirt of her dress up to free her legs as she ran wildly across the pasture.

Albert ran out to meet her.

Louella raced toward him and came up out of breath and still holding the hem of her dress in her hand.

"What you runnin . . ."

"You see them mens?"

"What mens?"

"In that car. Mister Mathis and Mister Jay. They drove back and forth on that road, lookin. They rid and rid, searchin over that house like they wantin somethin. Then they stop and Mister Mathis clam over the fence and come walkin. Then he turnt round and went back. I went out and they drove off?"

"Mister Mathis likely wantin know when I going pay him."

She turned her round eyes on him. "Worryin bout a debt ridin back and forth? Comin at that house till he seen me?"

"They just ridin, Mama. We go on back to the house."

"You better listen. Them mens up to somethin."

"I don't think they is."

"I been havin me a feelin, though."

He looked at her. Since Lettie had left he had noticed a change come over Louella. She went about her work brooding. She often sat on the porch and stared across the pasture. And at morning when the passenger train passed she sat dreamily, as though her thoughts moved down the track with the train. At night she turned in the bed, not sleeping.

"Anythin the matter?" he asked her one night.

"Ain't nothin."

Later, he sometimes heard her get out of bed and go sit in the kitchen.

Now, returning to the house with him, she said, "I wish we move off from here."

"Move, Mama?"

"I wish we do it. They ain't nothin round here but misery."

"But this where us live. This us home."

"You best say this just where us live. You know them white folks much as drove Sistah off from here."

"They sho ain't all to blame. She been restless. She been bound to go off, no tellin what."

"They drove her off. She been fraid bout what them folks going do. Them mens up to somethin, too."

Her words both pained and annoyed him. "Don't you believe Mister Tittle know what he doing? He told me go on with the house. And he been livin here long as anybody. Longer, I spec."

"You can't trust none of them folks. Don't you know that?"

"They some mens you can," he said, and he could hear the irritation that crept into his voice.

"I sho ain't seen none."

"I pend on Mister Tittle. I pend on what he say."

"You been livin long enough to know they word ain't good when they get cross and mad. But you go right on. You act like chillun. They knock you in yo head and you get up thinkin they give you a pat. How you going forget how they done to us? You know how they have shot and beat. My folks know it and yo folks, too. Both us folks, so's we can't forget how they have kilt and bled. But you has it in yo mind they good. Yo head don't make no sense to me, thinkin like it do."

"But this ain't no mob of folks, Mama. And folks dif'ent when they ain't gangin up in somethin. I believe what Mister Tittle say."

"You going learn. You best member Mister Tittle a white man fo he anythin. He may let you go head a piece, doing things, but he ain't going gainst them other folks. Mister Roberts ain't neither."

"They on us side, though."

"How you know what Mister Tittle thinkin? He ain't forgot you colored. First thing you know he going turn his back on you like you ain't no mo'n a dead snake in the road."

"Mister Tittle a man, Mama," he said, and did not try to hide his anger.

"You right, he a man." The thin lines gathered at the corners of her mouth. "A white man."

"It sho hurt me, seein you don't trust folks mo."

"They never give me nothin to trust them for."

"Some is. Some always is."

"Them mens just up to somethin. And you going see."

Albert ground a leaf into the dirt with the toe of his shoe. "Everythin be all right. But we got us some work to do, gettin that cotton. I be mighty glad could you help me some this e'nin. The boys pickin, and playin some, but I needin a real hand side of me."

She did not answer, but went inside the house, leaving him to wonder if he had convinced her of anything at all. On his way back to the field he noticed that the leaves of the sweet-gum tree had already turned yellow and orange and had begun to fall.

That night Albert went to bed early. But his back ached and an hour passed before he began to doze. When he finally fell asleep Louella still sat in her chair drawn up before the fireplace.

He did not know how long he had slept when a motion roused him. He rolled onto his side. As his senses came alive he was aware of Louella's sharp grip on his arm. She was shaking him.

"You want——"

"Shhh," she said, whispering.

He sat up wide awake. Louella sat up too and leaned toward him. "You hear that?"

"What is it, Mama?"

"They somethin out there."

They listened together while the darkness pressed against them close as water.

"I don't hear nothin."

"You listen."

A noise came then, from out near the lot. The sound was like the breaking of a dry twig.

"You hear it?"

"I hear somethin."

"Fo you woke up it been somebody walkin. It like they come from hind the garden."

Albert moved to get out of bed but Louella held him back. "Don't you go out there."

"My calf out there. I going see bout my calf."

She clutched his arm. "Listen."

The sound came again. A cool spot tingled on the back of Albert's neck; he hesitated. He waited only a moment, then pulled his arm from Louella's grasp and slipped out of bed. His chest tightened as he felt his way around the bed, quietly, with his hands out before him.

"You best don't go out there."

"Don't talk," he said.

He tried to discount the noise as he moved forward in the darkness, telling himself that the sound was probably made by a possum or a dog. And yet . . .

He made his way into the kitchen, moving close to the opened shutter, and looked out. Dimly he could see the shape of the sweet-gum tree and the outline of the shed. He heard the sound again. He believed it came from the far side of the lot. When he moved toward the door the loose boards creaked beneath his feet and he heard his heart beating loud.

He heard a small click and the cool spot on his neck moved upward to tighten his scalp against his head. He could not stop himself from shouting, "Who that? Who botherin my calf?"

"Papa!" It was Cooter, waking.

"Shhh," Louella said. "Shhh!"

A gun was fired. The flash, near the sweet-gum tree, blew a round orange hole in the darkness. Albert flinched.

"Papa!"

"Albert Clayton?" Louella called.

"You-all stay back," he said.

He jumped forward and his feet carried him headlong down the unseen steps. He ran across the yard, heading for the calf. When he jerked the lot gate open and stumbled to the shed the calf bleated. Albert's hands shook as he searched along the rafter above his head for the rope.

He found the rope and put it around the calf's neck and pulled the calf across the lot. The calf leaped and ran, jerking Albert, making him fall. But he was on his feet again in an instant, hurrying through the gate, back across the yard. He pulled the calf up the steps into the kitchen.

"Is you all right?"

"I bringin the calf in."

"You come on in here."

He looked out the back door. But he could see no movement and there was no sound except his heart rapping against his chest. He stood a moment more, away from the door, close against the wall now, with the calf held tight to his side. Even when he had argued strongest against Louella's doubts there had always lurked in the back of his mind the concern that Mister Mathis might do more than take a lien on the crop. He had never let Louella know this; he knew he must not now, and when in an urgent voice she said, "Who shot?" he answered calmly, "I don't know, Mama. It just somebody out there huntin. Huntin them possums, I reckon. I hear they dogs runnin."

He squared his feet, pushing his weight down on his heels. And when her voice came again, filled with the fright he wanted to stop, saying, "I don't hear no dogs. It them mens done that," he tried to speak as though of some half-forgotten detail of their lives: "It just somebody huntin. They dogs out there in the woods right now. But I going keep the calf here in the house. So's they won't scare him."

While he led the calf across the floor and tied him to the foot of the bed, he wondered if Louella had believed his lie. She did not say anything, and in the silence that followed, the house itself seemed to lift in quietness and hold itself poised as on unseen hands. He tried to see Louella's face. But she had moved; he saw her pass like a shadow toward the bed.

"You-all get in the bed with Mama," he told Cooter and Daniel.

Albert drew a chair close beside the calf and sat alert, thinking. Sometimes, in the hours that followed, his back tingled as though the shot had just been fired again. When the feeling passed he heard Louella toss in the bed. He knew she did not sleep, and he felt as though her eyes fastened some question on him. And in the darkness he sought her eyes too, with his answer.

SIXTEEN

"I'VE BEEN WATCHING them all summer long," Mister Tittle said. "They're just trying to scare you."

Mister Tittle turned his head to look across his yard, beyond the crape-myrtle bushes that stood brown-leafed in the early sun, and fixed his eyes on some distant spot over by the railroad tracks. He folded his hands over one knee and did not speak for so long a time that Albert believed Mister Tittle's mind had become engaged with some other thoughts.

But Mister Tittle spoke again at last. "If they had been dead set on stopping you, they could have done it. And long before now. Maybe, God helping, they're about to see what they've been doing to this town. Maybe that sawmill moving off from here has made them pause to think.

"Mathis may still not be thinking. Maybe he's just missing business. But for whatever reason he's held back, not done some bastard thing, it will leave its scar on him. A scar on this town, too, that'll take a long time for people to forget. Not because of you and the house, though that's what they'll say. But because they've had to open their eyes against their own stubborn wills."

"Yessir."

"Maybe Mathis and the others aren't holding back for any reason at all." For a moment Mister Tittle sat withdrawn, as though his eyes turned inward to look on some secret thing. "But I don't believe it's a fight they want. I may be wrong. It depends on what you want to do."

"They ain't hurt that calf none, Mister Tittle."

"Then don't let them scare you. Goddamn. Ten, fifteen years ago they'd already have done some devilish thing. They wouldn't have waited and they wouldn't fool around shooting at a calf. For less reason than now I've seen them get their guns and tell a man to get out of town in twelve hours or they'd kill him. They meant it, too. And people knew they meant it. Men ran, leaving crop, wife and children to root hog or die. You remember when they beat Silas Rawlins with a horsewhip, in the woods behind the Dickens place. Because of an eight-dollar debt.

He died within a week. They shot Elza Crosby in the leg three times, made him get away from here. But they haven't done anything like that now. Maybe times change in spite of people. Maybe it changes most because of the people who don't want it to change at all. I've told you what I think about it and you can do what you want to do. But, God, man, get that cotton out! It'll soon be October. Mathis may need the money we owe him, too. We'll want to pay him as soon as we can."

Albert went back to the tenant house reassured. He sat on the back steps a long time while Louella stood behind him, waiting. Sometimes she moved back and forth, trying to get his attention. He still wanted her to believe the shot had been fired by hunters and he kept silent. But when she spoke he knew that she had seen through his lie.

"What he say bout it?"

"Say they just tryin scare me. Say they ain't going do no mo."

"That man done start lyin to you. Now he has. He know well as me them mens likely beat you and run you off from here one night."

"Mister Tittle say times change. Say they ain't going do no mo."

"How he know?"

"Mister Tittle know what he sayin."

"You ain't going make no clear money from the cotton noways, cause of them debts. But that calf going make it you get me and them chillun and yo'self in sho enough trouble. That very calf . . ."

He waited, thinking she would talk on, but she did not speak again.

During the days that followed, people came to the field to visit and to deal out like cards their words of dismay or advice. For news of the shot being fired had blown over Longfield like a sudden wind, and formed a question. They all felt obliged to take the question into their fingers and turn it before their eyes like a wheel. And as with a wheel they always found themselves come back to that point from which they had started. Those who had been proudest when Albert estimated the paint were the first to have their doubts that he should go on with his plan. Others argued that he must; so they passed the question about among themselves, with an air of solemn perplexity, until finally it grew too heavy for their hands to hold. It was then that they came visiting.

"They ain't hit the calf?"

"They ain't, Minnie Sue. Just put some shot in the shed."

A pause, and then: "I glad they ain't hit him, Prince. It please me know it. I happy you going go on with yo house."

Later, at Mister Tittle's barn:

"You best be ticular. You sho had. They may just givin you a warnin. But it make me mighty proud if'n you go on. Too many folks done run when they ought to just sot."

"You right, R.A."

And behind the tenant house, at the edge of the garden, in the dark:

"You give up that notion, fo they do somethin serious. They ain't no folks to stop somethin once they got it start. A man just got to use his head."

Others came the following day at odd hours, bringing their wishes and their doubts. Louella listened closely to all who spoke but she did not say anything to Albert.

"Mama?"

He wanted to hear her voice, to talk to her of any small thing that would bring her near to him.

"Mama?"

She turned away, as though she did not hear.

On Sunday afternoon, after Cooter and Daniel had gone into the woods to hunt possum grapes, Albert sat with Louella on the porch. It was a cool day for early October; full signs of autumn were in the air. The leaves had fallen from the sweet-gum tree, the pasture was spotted with brown patches of grass and the swallows did not spread their quick wings against the sky any more. The sky itself held a tint of grayness. And on the horizon some soft white clouds sat still as old men thinking.

On the lane Preacher Tom's car came into sight. The preacher had been to the tenant house only once since Lettie had left—to inquire when Lettie planned to leave Augustus and come home. In the car with the preacher were R-Rula and Solo Thompson.

"You-all get out," Albert said.

They all sat on the porch while the sun, behind them, threw the shadow of the house across the yard at their feet.

"I reckon you bout got yo cotton out," Preacher Tom said. His voice was like a whisper from another room.

"We is, Preacher Tom. Going finish it up on a Monday, they don't nothin happen."

"You make much this year, Prince?" Solo said.

"We going get six bale. Maybe little mo'n that. But them debts going bout take it all."

"Ain't been such a good year."

They spoke of the weather for a time, announcing to themselves the season upon them, but Albert could tell they all talked with other thoughts on their minds. He looked at Preacher Tom and waited.

Several minutes passed before Preacher Tom cleared his throat. "We hear them talkin bout the shot, Prince."

Albert nodded.

"You know it ain't my natural way go shovin in yo business. It sho ain't. But they some folks ain't so sho it right you go on with yo plannin. They some folks done thought deep bout things, dug in they heads far down. And they folks got yo good in they heart."

Solo and R-Rula nodded, as if by some signal.

"'Tween some of us we know you headin yo'self to misery. We wantin help you void that, if'n we can. So we come here with our feelin."

Preacher Tom left the porch and stood in the yard, facing the house as though about to deliver a sermon.

Louella, sitting attentive, looked at Albert, who sat

leaning forward, his feet flat on the floor and his head turned downward.

"Folks think a heap of you," Preacher Tom began. "They do. And they hate to see you takin riskies. You got yo chillun and Louella to think bout. If'n they somethin happen to you, the Lawd would see them in want and need. You have to think on that, give it some long thought. I see it my duty, talkin to folks, knowin, to come down here to yo house and say: 'Watch how you go on, Prince, fo you get yo'-self hurt.' It look to me I heard from everybody round here the call to say it, come down here and speak with you.

"R-Rula there, and Solo—" he motioned toward them—"think the same as me. And I told them we would get in the car and come down to you. And tell you what we found deep in us head."

"It just what we thinkin," R-Rula said.

"It is," Solo said, and took himself a dip of snuff from the lid of a small round snuffbox.

A silence followed, and in that silence Albert thought of his father and his father's father; thought, too, of his sons and the sons of his sons to come. He stood.

"I been thinkin a heap mo'n you-all know,

Preacher Tom. They no way of tellin fo sho if'n them mens do somethin mo. But I going on. They ain't nothin mo to do but that. And I is been thinkin of Mama and them boys."

He felt his jaw tighten. "You-all s'prise me, Preacher Tom. Feelin the way you do's. They some things you-all ain't seein."

R-Rula and Solo exchanged a quick glance and got off the porch as though moved by a single pair of legs. They gathered close to Preacher Tom, who stood with his head shaking in little motions. Together their six eyes held Albert as a flashlight beam holds a spot of darkness. On their faces showed the certain knowledge that they beheld a man both stubborn and wicked, a man willing to sacrifice his wife and his sons to a notion that was both simple and profound.

"We tryin save you leavin," Solo said.

"And bringin misery on yo house," R-Rula said.

"Rilin folks," Preacher Tom said.

Albert looked at them steadily, one by one. "I know you-all mean well," he said. "And I thank you for comin. But I ruther you-all don't say no mo. Mama already upsot. I ruther you-all just get in the car and go on. Leave me and Mama lone."

Preacher Tom lifted his hand. "We ain't meant no harm. We . . ."

But Albert turned from them and went inside.

"You-all see," Louella said.

"A shame fo us Lawd," Preacher Tom said.

Their voices came in to Albert where he sat in the bedroom. But soon the car started and moved up the lane and Louella's footsteps sounded on the floor.

"Mama?"

The footsteps stopped; he saw her pause at the door.

"Come in here with me."

She went into the kitchen, where he found her sitting beside the stove with the butcher knife in her hand. He studied her face. She appeared to be tired, as though she had not slept for a long time. And he noticed that her shoulders were rounded, bent, held down as though by some great weight.

"Don't you listen to them."

"You better listen yo'self. Think some bout yo'-self, and me and them chillun. You got no business runnin folks off like that."

"Preacher Tom and them don't have no understandin of some things. They some things they don't know."

"You yet hopin, ain't you?"

"A man out hope worser off than Old Bertha, Mama. She least lookin to find her another calf fo long."

"Preacher Tom and them know them folks. Know how it get in they head to beat and run. Them mens just waitin——"

"You said that enough, now. Don't talk that-a-way."

"You ain't going listen, I going least talk how I want to. Them mens——"

"Hush, Mama."

"I ain't going hush. Seem to me like sometime you ain't got no sense a-tall."

"I told you hush, now. Mister Tittle——"

"Mister Tittle foolin you mo'n anybody. He lettin you go on when he know better. He worser than Mister Mathis and the others."

With a single step he was beside her. He felt his fingers dig into the soft flesh of her arms as he spun her, fixing her before him, making her face him. He saw her eyes grow round, and under the tight grip of his hands her arms grew limp and the knife fell to the floor between their feet.

"Can't you see? Can't you——"

"Turn me loose!"

She turned her head but he forced it back to face his own. His voice thickened. "You can't let yo hate make you can't see. Yo hate makin you blind. The same way Mister Tittle say Mister Mathis doing."

"Let me loose!" She kicked him against the shin so hard that he freed her and stepped back. She fled into the bedroom.

His fingers shook and an emptiness welled up inside him. The emptiness gave way to a feeling of pain. He stood a moment, then picked her comb up from the floor where it had fallen and took it in to the bed where she lay with her head buried in her arms.

"Here yo comb."

She did not move to take the comb, but he tucked it into her hair anyway and put his hand on her shoulder. He felt that he must do some small thing for her, so that she would know that he regretted speaking harshly. He remembered the knife, which she had taken from the shelf for him to sharpen, and he went back to the kitchen to get the file from above the door. In a short time he had the long blade filed sharp as a razor. He ran his thumb lightly over the fine edge, testing his work, then put the knife aside and looked out the back door.

The sun outlined the tops of the pine trees clearly, like dark figures pasted on yellow paper. And beyond the garden, not very high, he could make out the branches of the wild-plum tree and the close fruit hanging purple as ripe muscadines. When he sat on the steps he became aware of a shadow that stole slowly across the yard, pushed toward him by the declining sun.

An hour passed and the shadow had reached his feet before Louella came into the kitchen for a dipper of water. He took the knife up from the floor beside him.

"I sharpen it for you, Mama. It cut that meat good, now."

She took the knife without looking at him, put it on the shelf behind the stove and left the kitchen. He heard the mattress on the bed make a dry noise and knew that she lay down again.

He sat thoughtful while the shadow moved past the top of his shoes. The shadow moved quickly now, urged by the sun that he could no longer see, and when some minutes later the shade had covered him and filled the door he thought he heard Daniel and Cooter calling him. But the voices he heard came from over on the road, where some children were walking.

He sat on, but soon the silence of the house became more than he could bear. He made a noise on the step, to signal to Louella that he had gone, and walked out into the pasture.

SEVENTEEN

TUESDAY NIGHT after supper Albert sat on the wood-box beside the stove. He had finished picking the cotton late in the afternoon, but he was thinking about the calf now, trying to decide on a day to take the calf to the auction.

"Friday might do," he said aloud.

Before him Louella bent over the table to brush some crumbs into the palm of her hand. He tried to get her attention.

Louella paused a moment, standing very still, before she took the butcher knife up from the table and held it before her thoughtfully. Then, quickly, she crossed the kitchen to place the knife carefully on the shelf behind the stove.

"I could take him on a Friday. He already weighin mo'n four hundred. Mister Tittle say he think the calf going bring enough to buy the paint. I going need me a brush, too. So's I . . ."

Louella's lips parted for some outburst. She clenched her hand against her side and stared at him. Her lips came together grimly and with effort she held her tongue.

He lifted his shoulders, getting ready to speak, but before he formed his words she turned quick as a cat and ran from the kitchen. Her steps clicked across the loose boards of the front porch and ceased abruptly as she went into the yard. For a moment he sat too surprised to follow, but he collected himself and went swiftly toward the door. Before he leaped off the porch his lifted foot caught in mid-air. A sensation seized him, sending a painful little tingle down the small of his back. He brought his foot against the floor with a loud thump and made himself stand perfectly still while he studied the darkness. Louella was not in sight and he strained his ears to catch some sound of her. But he heard only the distant rumble of a freight train far away down the track and above that sound the loud hooting of an owl somewhere on the creek.

He went into the bedroom. The lamplight shone bright against his face, but he noticed how the glow faded as it traveled outward, growing faint as twilight at the foot of the bed and giving no light at all to the back corners of the room. He felt as though he sat in the center of a circle whose outer edge lay covered with night. And all at once he knew another urge to plunge into that darkness, to follow Louella, but a feeling deeper than this impulse held him in the full glare of the lamp.

He stared at the chair opposite him, pulled up before the hearth directly beneath the mantel, as if for someone to sit. His eyes held fixed while outside he heard the faint scratching sound of some dry sweetgum leaves being swept across the yard. Somewhere a shutter banged closed, then swung open, squeaking on its rusted hinges. The noise had not died away when a shadow flipped over the chair. Albert sat erect with a start. There beside him the old woman appeared in the chair as always, with her hands folded across her formless lap, with the brown snuff juice running along the little cracks of her wrinkled chin. She leaned her head forward, as though to whisper, and he heard the words: "Death be's a little man, and he go from do' to do'. But they mo. They mo you got to know."

The light trembled again, more violently now,

and other shadows, tall as men, flickered back and forth against the walls. Albert stood quickly and after a second of complete stillness he slowly placed his hand flat on the straw-woven seat of the chair. He let out a short breath. The chair was empty, as he knew it had been empty since he entered the room. A wind had been slipping through the opened shutter to stir the flame of the lamp, making the shadows, and for a moment his mind had played a trick on him. He nodded and sat down again.

For a time, in the silence that followed, he thought about the old woman's words. He turned the words over in his head, this way and that, trying to dig up their meaning. He fixed his attention on the words from all angles and even pictured the old woman when she had first uttered them. But finally he had to let out a grunt of disgust with himself for not understanding. He leaned back in his chair and gave himself up to the silence of the room.

An hour passed before Louella returned. She paused at the door with her hands on her hips as though debating whether to come in or go out again.

"A wind risin," he said.

"A wind?"

"It risin."

He tried to see her face clearly.

But she dropped onto the bed as though tired out in all her body. He did not want her to be angry again, so he did not pry into where she had been.

"The wind sho risin," he said again. And at that moment a gust of wind whipped in, the shutter above his head banged closed and the lamp went out. He waited until his eyes grew accustomed to the dark before he made his way to the bed.

Albert was up the following morning long before Mister Tittle's rooster crowed of coming daylight. From the adjoining room he heard talking: Daniel and Cooter arguing with each other. Albert knew they had been awake for over an hour, restless for the adventure of riding the cotton truck to the gin. They stood dressed and waiting for him when he went into the kitchen, and they crowded close at his heels while he built a fire in the stove.

"Is the truck come, Papa?" Cooter said.

"I hear it," Daniel said, and cocked his head to one side to listen. "I hear it comin now."

"I don't reckon that it yet," Albert said, "but it be on here fo long."

"You going take me, ain't you, Papa?" Daniel said.

He turned his round eyes up to Albert. "You took Cooter that last time."

Albert put some water on the stove to boil and measured out four tablespoons of coffee. "Somebody have to stay with Mama. And water and feed the calf."

"Cooter know that calf better'n me. Don't you, Cooter?"

"Hold yo talkin, boy!" Cooter scolded, and moved to the opposite side of Albert from Daniel. "Can't us both go, Papa?"

"That three bale of cotton going fill the truck. And Mister Roberts always got them folks wantin to ride. Then too, that leave Mama lone. And she need her a man bout the house."

Albert poured water into the coffeepot and watched Cooter from the corner of his eye. The boy had turned away and walked to the back door, where the first gray light of dawn came in. Cooter held his fingers hooked into the bib of his overalls and his full lips moved, as though he held some argument with himself. At last he turned back to the kitchen and looked at Daniel with a superior air.

"I stay then, Papa."

Louella came into the kitchen and took the cup

of coffee Albert offered her. The lines that curved around her mouth were distinct this morning, like the small veins of a leaf, and the corners of her mouth turned downward. Albert thought she looked sadder than he had ever seen her, as if the trial of years had finally welled into the softness of her cheeks to burden her with their sorrow. He saw her hand tremble.

"You want me bring you anythin from Gibbsburg, Mama?"

She shook her head in reply.

He had already poured himself a second cup of coffee when he heard the truck coming down the lane.

"Cooter, go yonder and tell Mister Tittle I comin."

Cooter and Daniel plunged out the back door yelling to each other to move out of the way.

"You going take them with you?" Louella said.

"I going take Daniel. Cooter say he stay."

"Cooter can help you mo on the truck."

"Daniel want to go mighty bad. He ain't been down there."

"I know he ain't, but he might could get hurt on that truck. Foolin round that gin. I ruther he stay here with me."

For a moment he hesitated. But her concern pleased him, it brought her nearer to him, and though he hated to disappoint Daniel, he nodded. "He might could get hurt. I tell him stay here with you. Tell him give the calf some water if'n we don't get back fo dinner. I going leave the calf shut up in the stall while I gone."

He could feel her eyes follow him when he went down the steps and headed for the lot. Beside the stall he paused to look at the calf.

"Don't you get out this stall," he said. "I don't want you runnin bout that pastah, throwin yo weight off fo I take you down yonder. You worth fifty dollar and that a big piece of money for a bully calf like you." He turned away and strode across the pasture toward the truck, where Mister Tittle's voice lifted impatiently.

The light of day came slowly. The land lay overcast with clouds as far as the eye could see. When the cotton was loaded and the truck pulled up the lane, Albert saw Louella standing in the front yard. The gray walls of the house rose behind her starkly, darker than the sky. He looked at her intently, seeing the dim outline of her figure standing fixed amid a grayness that held her and the house, held the day it-self, in a stilled composite pose like a picture.

The picture imprinted itself on his mind as though inked there with a pen. When the truck reached Gibbsburg and pulled into line to get onto the gin ramp, the scene remained boldly before him and he did not climb down to join the men who gathered in little groups to joke and discuss the price of cot-ton. He was aware that at the back of the gin bales of cotton tumbled out, compressed, sacked and belted, were hooked and wheeled away along the platform, but this activity did not make him quicken with ex-citement now as it usually did. For he sat held by another hour, another place, and by a familiar figure dimly seen. He lifted a lock of cotton to hold it be-fore him, stretched it slowly, removed the seed and let it drop into a small pile at his feet.

The truck soon moved onto the ramp and the suc-tion feed drew the cotton up with a roar. But beyond the roar, beyond the hum of the gin and the shouting of working men, he thought he heard another voice come on the wind that blew about his head. Even when Mister Tittle had sold the cotton and took Albert aside to pay him the seventeen dollars and ten cents he had cleared after his debts, Albert could not rid himself of an odd feeling of concern.

"We ain't going stay long, is we, Mister Tittle?"

"God, Prince, you usually like to spend the day. You in a hurry?"

"Yessir. Soon's you ready."

But Mister Tittle had to attend to business. Albert waited, while in his mind the picture of Louella standing before the tenant house waited too, as though for him to discover in it something he had not seen before. He noticed Cooter standing beside him, looking at him puzzled.

"Here you a dime." He extended the coin. "You may can find you some ice cream there at the corner."

He watched Cooter cross the street, saw him disappear into the rear door of the drugstore, before he clasped his hands tightly before him and settled to wait. It seemed to him he had never waited so long. His urge to depart, at once, aroused in him a tenseness physical and acute, made the calves of his legs quiver with a tingling ache. He stretched his legs out as Cooter climbed back into the truck.

"You want some, Papa?" He offered the ice-cream cone.

Albert gazed at the cone, seeing the white drops melt over the brown edge, wiggle downward and form a round spot against Cooter's hand.

"Papa? You want some?"

Albert shook his head and turned again to scan the street for a sight of Mister Tittle. But thirty minutes passed before Mister Tittle came up.

"We going now, ain't we, Mister Tittle?"

"I think we're about ready."

Albert stood behind the cab of the truck, facing forward into the wind that whistled about his ears and burned his eyes. The tingling ache still lingered in his legs. His knees ached too, with the desire to run, and his thoughts kept leaping ahead along the road, moving faster than the truck. He could hear his heart pounding when finally the truck stopped in front of Mister Tittle's house.

He jumped to the ground as Mister Tittle opened the door and spoke.

"Do you want to take the calf tomorrow, Prince? We could get the truck again."

"Can't we take him on a Friday, Mister Tittle?" The words came quickly; he wanted to hurry on to the house.

Mister Tittle spoke into the cab of the truck, then

nodded. "That's all right. Be ready about eight. The auction . . ."

But Albert turned, not hearing, and without waiting for Cooter started walking toward the lane.

"Well, I'm . . ." Albert did not stop and Mister Tittle's voice faded.

Once beyond the barn, with the gate fastened behind him, Albert began to run down the lane. All the time he ran he kept his eyes on the house, though he saw no one there. But just then he saw Daniel on the pasture, coming to meet him. When they drew near Albert slowed his pace to look into the boy's face.

"Papa! Mama . . ."

Albert did not wait for Daniel to finish speaking, but dashed into the house. He stopped, listening, before he called Louella's name.

There was no answer, no sound at all except his own quick breathing. He went from room to room but the dim cool light of the house gave up no sign of Louella. He dropped into a chair beside the kitchen stove, where Louella so often sat, and he remained there motionless and perplexed until Daniel came in.

"Yo calf, Papa . . . Mama . . ."

Albert jumped up and with Daniel running behind went to the lot. The lot gate was chained, as always, the crib door closed, all as he had left it early that morning. But when he reached the stall and stopped beside it his breathing ceased and his hand gripped the top board of the stall until his knuckles widened, separate and prominent.

The calf lay on his side with his head stretched forward. His hind legs were thrust backward and his front legs crumpled awkwardly beneath his body. The round eyes, fixed in their wild stare, were like fogged glass, and a foam like pink soap lather stood on the nostrils where some black flies crawled. A pool of dirty blood larger than a washtub had formed on the ground. At the edge of the pool the blood had mixed with dust and caked, drying. The kitchen knife lay in the blood where it had been dropped.

He had sharpened the knife. He remembered that as, from his stooped position, he looked upward. Cloud, fixed in the jagged hole of the stall's roof like a swatch of gray cloth patched on, met his gaze, near and oppressive. He looked back at the calf, straightened up, as a sound half cry and half curse escaped his lips. He clenched his fist.

"Mama start to cryin when you went off, Papa," Daniel said. The boy's voice sounded faint, as if it came from a great distance. "Cryin and——"

"Where she gone to?"

"Cross the pastah to'ad the . . ."

But Albert turned back through the gate to the pasture, walking swiftly toward the creek. At the point where the road sloped to the narrow shallows he stopped shortly. From far away, from a direction he could not determine, he believed he heard some-one call.

EIGHTEEN

ALBERT LOOKED to his right along the edge of the creek beyond the wild-plum tree and to his left where the young grove of pines grew. He waited to hear the call again, but it did not come and he turned to his right, cutting through the woods where grape and muscadine vines hung thickly, the quickness that welled inside him drawing his feet surely through bramble briers, over fallen limbs, around thick clumps of underbrush.

Though he searched closely, he did not see Louella. He retraced his steps, going back along the creek below the crossing, toward the grove of pines. The path he followed dipped down, curving, winding its way through woods silent as in early morning before the sun rose. Just now, somewhere ahead of him, a single acorn fell to make a dull heavy sound that spread out in waves growing wider and fainter, like the liquid round ripples made by a stone dropped into still water. He mounted a small incline and went toward the gate that led into the field. And now he saw Louella standing far beyond the cotton house, against the distant fringe of trees. She stood quietly, not catching sight of him, but a moment later she moved from the edge of the trees and once out of their shadow her figure outlined itself against the wide sweep of gray sky.

He stopped and fastened his eyes on her.

Her body bent slightly forward, as if she might be leaning against a wind, the posture bringing to his mind memories of her before the stove, bending to stir boiling collards or to lift the hot coffeepot.

He stood motionless, but on his temple a vein began to throb quick and hard as the tap of a small hammer.

Just now Louella turned. Seeing him, her fingers touched the loose folds of her blue dress, as if she tried to steady herself. Their eyes caught, holding each other, while overhead the gray clouds thinned, changing, making the ragged tops of the trees stand out sharply. Neither of them moved, as if sight itself wedded them over the distance.

Moments passed before Albert began, slowly, to

walk toward her. He saw her lift her arm slightly, as though she, too, might start forward. Her gesture, when she moved her arm, reminded him of the manner in which the old woman had motioned vaguely over the room the day she died. He remembered the old woman's words. Remembering, he stopped so shortly that his heels dug into the ground. His body trembled and he drew in a breath so deep that his shoulders tightened uncomfortably inside his jumper.

A second later, quickly, his whole body alive to his steps, he went across the field.

Louella began to walk toward him. The distance between them narrowed, grew shorter still, until at last, two rows apart, standing face to face, they stopped. He noticed a streak of blood across the hem of her dress. The sight of it made the quickness well again, stronger than ever now. He took a step toward her.

Her lips quivered as she drew her hand across her hip. But she did not move and he saw the lines gather tightly around the corners of her mouth.

His anger flared. He wanted to shake her by the shoulders. But he could not bring his hands from his side. He did not need to, for, without warning, tears appeared in her eyes. He was waiting when she flung herself against him. His anger left and he held her quietly, while over her head he saw the field stretch away.

Autumn, a lonely time in the Piney Woods, was upon the earth now. But though the earth had grown gray again, Albert saw nothing final in an empty cotton boll on a bare brown stalk. For in autumn the bark of the pine trees turned dark as old leather, and the pine needles deepened their color, preparing for the season ahead when they would glisten in the sunshine as always and send their whisper over the land.

He took Louella by the arm and they walked across the creek to the pine tree that was the tallest to be seen for miles. He could remember her standing beside the tree only once before, briefly one day in summer. He had not noticed her then, but today he saw that she rested easily, as he often stood.

Quietly she studied him for a long time, as if seeing him clearly for the first time. "I ruint yo chance to paint the house." It made him happy to hear her words come freely. "Cause I been fraid for you and me and them chillun."

"They been plenty make you feel like that. And Preacher Tom and them, too."

He stepped back from the tree so that he could

get a better view of her beside it. The old woman's words came into his mind again, and though he saw Louella standing alone, she did not appear solitary to him. Near her, uncertain, stood some of his own people. But behind them, original, were the white men who did not understand what a white house could mean, who had in their old wrongness killed the calf more surely than Louella. Seeing them all, Albert could not forget too that in his love he had sharpened the knife. But from the stilled fullness of the hour a new knowing came to him: he realized that one beginning had led him to yet another. There would be a new beginning.

Louella drew his attention. "But you been going right on, face of all. Till I——"

"They a lot in us life make us do things," he broke in, not wanting her to linger on the past. "Sometime cause we don't know somethin. But then sometime just cause we think somethin of somebody."

There was a brightness in the steady gaze she gave him. "We get the house painted next year," she said.

"We will."

Later, when they walked across the pasture toward the tenant house, Cooter and Daniel ran to meet them.

"I hungry," Daniel said.

"It time for us dinner." Cooter spoke sadly, his eyes turned toward the lot.

Albert looked at Cooter, saw the firm muscles that had come into his son's arms during the year, the strength he saw growing that made him proud. "Cooter get some wood, Mama cook us somethin."

"I get it!" Daniel cried.

"You can't tote no wood, boy," Cooter said, and he began a race with Daniel toward the woodpile.

"Cooter think he can do mo'n anybody," Louella said.

"He growin so."

They did not look toward the stall where the calf lay, though Albert told himself he must bury the calf the following day. But his mind did not dwell on this and he found himself already thinking of the coming year. Winter would be short, and soon the dark solid earth would roll to the point of his plow again. When that time came he would have Louella beside him, and his sons, and he would get him another calf and would go to his fields again, to plant his cotton.

He followed Louella up the steps and helped her build a fire in the stove. Soon the kitchen held the warm smell of food, and while she cooked he went to sit in the bedroom.

A few moments later a rain began to fall. It was late-October rain, and in the quietness of his thoughts he saw it slanting across his fields, falling on the cotton rows, giving new life to the land. He nodded to himself.

Above his head the raindrops fell softly on the tin roof, making their quiet music, their sound giving to the room its old comfort.

THE END

The writer expresses his appreciation to the Eugene F. Saxton Memorial Trust.